To Alison —

Love
in the
Light

LAURA KAYE

Let your light shine!

xo Laura Kaye

Love in the Light
FIRST EDITION January 2016
LOVE IN THE LIGHT © Laura Kaye.
ALL RIGHTS RESERVED.

ISBN 978-1522863915

The characters and events portrayed in this book are fictional and/or are used fictitiously and are solely the product of the author's imagination. Any similarity to persons living or dead, places, businesses, events, or locales is purely coincidental.

Front Cover Art by Tricia "Pickyme" Schmitt
Back Cover and Interior by The Killion Group

PRAISE FOR *LOVE IN THE LIGHT*

"Readers that have been anxiously waiting for more of this story will be thrilled with the passionate and poignant way Kaye dives back in with this complicated and much loved couple. *Love in the Light* will have readers falling in love with Caden and Makenna all over again!"

~ Jay Crownover, New York Times Bestselling Author of the Marked Men Series

"This follow up to one of the most beloved couples in romance is delivered in the emotional and touching way that only Laura Kaye can do. *Love in the Light* is everything I could have wanted for Makenna and Caden—and more!"

~ Jillian Stein, Read-Love-Blog

"Sexy, emotional and incredibly heartwarming, fans of Laura Kaye won't be disappointed!"

~ Monica Murphy, New York Times Bestselling Author of the One Week Girlfriend Quartet

"Laura Kaye has a gift for writing beautifully damaged men and Caden Grayson leads the pack with enough vulnerability to twist your heart in knots."

~ Tessa Bailey, New York Times Bestselling Author of the Line of Duty Series

"This book *delivers* - sweet romance, smoking hot sex, an entire tissue box full of angsty drama, and such love shining off the pages that it will blind you."

~ Christi Barth, Author of the Shore Secrets Series

HOT CONTEMPORARY ROMANCE BY LAURA KAYE

Hard Ink Series
HARD AS IT GETS
HARD AS YOU CAN
HARD TO HOLD ON TO
HARD TO COME BY
HARD TO BE GOOD
HARD TO LET GO
HARD AS STEEL
HARD EVER AFTER
HARD TO SERVE

Hearts in Darkness Duet
HEARTS IN DARKNESS
LOVE IN THE LIGHT

Heroes Series
HER FORBIDDEN HERO
ONE NIGHT WITH A HERO

Raven Riders Series
RIDE HARD
RIDE ROUGH

Stand Alone Titles
DARE TO RESIST
JUST GOTTA SAY

When the cloud in the sky starts to pour
And your life is just a storm you're braving
Don't tell yourself you can't lean on someone else
Cause we all need saving
Sometimes

~Jon McLaughlin
We All Need Saving

DEDICATION

To Lea, Christi, Jillian, and Liz for giving me courage.

To Marcy for telling me I had to do this.

To BK and the girls for helping me get it done.

To all the readers who asked if there would be more.

This is for you, with all of my heart.

CHAPTER ONE

Makenna James gasped awake, rushing up from sleep as if being tugged from deep under water. What had woken her—

Caden moaned next to her, thrashing against the pillow, a cold sweat on his forehead. Her heart already raced from being startled, but now it squeezed for a whole other reason.

She pulled herself closer and stroked her hand over the deep scar that jagged from his temple to the back of his head. A beam of early morning sunlight filtered through the window next to her bed, revealing his furrowed brow and clenched jaw. God, she hated the way his subconscious tormented him. "Caden? Hey, it's okay. Wake up."

Startled brown eyes flashed to her, not quite tracking for a long moment. "Red?" A scowl settled onto his gorgeous face when awareness returned to him. "Dammit. Sorry," he said, voice like gravel.

She smiled and shook her head, still stroking the close-shaved brown hair surrounding his scar the way he liked. "Nothing to be sorry for."

His arms came around her and he shifted her on top of his broad bare chest, her legs settling over his naked hips. "Damn nightmare." Caden blew out a breath. "I hate this. For you."

"I've got you." Makenna kissed him, reveling as she always did in the nip of his metal spider bite piercings against her lips. *And I love you.* Though she kept that thought to herself.

She'd realized weeks ago that she'd fallen for him, irrevocably and all the way, but she'd never given voice to the words. Something inside her warned against letting him know—yet—just how serious her feelings had become. Not because she believed Caden didn't care for her, too. A part of her worried that making a man so marked by loss confront how close they'd become might freak him out.

Fourteen years had passed since he'd lost his mother and younger brother Sean in a car accident that had trapped and injured Caden and left him claustrophobic, scarred, and alone, and the memory of it still tortured him. As the nightmare proved. "Don't you worry about it."

"You're too damn good for me," Caden rasped, deepening the kiss, his big hands digging into her sleep-mussed red hair, his body coming alive beneath hers.

It wasn't the first time he'd said something along those lines, and the sentiment always made the center of her chest ache. How could he not see what she saw—a strong, amazing man who'd dedicated his life to helping others? "Never," she whispered around the edge of the kiss. "You're everything to me."

Her words unleashed a groan from deep in his throat. Caden lifted his head and pursued her lips, nipping and tugging and sucking until Makenna was hot and needy.

The nightmares didn't come every night. They mostly surfaced when Caden was stressed out over something. It didn't take much to guess what today's stressor might be—their trip to Philadelphia to see her father and brothers for Thanksgiving. The holiday was as close to sacred as things got in her family, her father insisting all four of his kids make their way home to give thanks for all they had in their lives, family most especially.

No way she could go without Caden, though. Not when his family was gone. And not when her heart demanded that Caden was family, too.

When she'd first brought up the trip, he'd actually thought she intended to go without him, and even said he'd just volunteer to work so the guys at the firehouse who had families could have off. Makenna made it clear that she wanted him to come with her, and she'd probably never seen him more resemble a deer in the headlights. Which she totally got it. Meeting someone's family for the first, time was never easy. But once he'd seen how much spending the day together meant to her, he'd agreed like the sweet, sweet man he was. And so they were road-tripping it for a weekend of turkey, stuffing, and football with the testosterone-dominated James clan.

Caden's grip tightened in her hair as his hips surged beneath her. "I have to get in you. Do we have time? Please tell me there's time."

She smiled against his lips, the thick desire in his voice rushing heat through her veins. Grinding her core against his hard length, she said, "As long as we're quick." Though, truth be told, it wouldn't take much to convince her to linger in this man's arms. She was that far gone and he was that freaking hot.

A sound like a growl rumbled from Caden's throat. "Thanksgiving feasts are meant to be savored," he said, flipping them over and pinning her to the mattress. He helped her remove her panties and his Station 7 shirt with his last name 'GRAYSON' on the back. She'd long ago stolen it from him to sleep in—much to his satisfaction. And then he held himself above her and rocked his erection against the very place where she needed him most.

Makenna nodded. "I agree, but I'd rather not have to explain to my brothers why we were late." Which would be a total nightmare. They'd be like a pack of lions fighting over a meaty carcass, not giving up until they'd made her spill. Then, like the pains in the asses they could be, they'd spend the day making up all the juicy bits she wouldn't tell them to embarrass her—and Caden. No way was she letting that happen. Caden was nervous enough.

His expression darkened and his eyes shuttered, just a bit. Enough to reveal just how anxious he was about the trip.

"I want you, Caden," she said, hoping to pull him back from wherever he'd gone. She stroked her fingers down his strong back. "And I need you. However I can have you."

The shadows disappeared from his face and he finally nodded and quirked a half smile. "Hard and fast it is, then."

Yes, please!

He reached to the nightstand and pulled a condom from the drawer, then sat back to roll it on.

"Love it hard and fast," she whispered, watching him. Her gaze raked over the cut muscles of his chest and stomach and traced down from the yellow rose tattoo on his left pec to the large black tribal that wrapped around his side. Everything about him—his ink, his piercings, even his scars—was so damn sexy.

"Then hold on tight." The words had barely spilled from his lips before he was right there, probing her entrance, pushing into her, filling her with that delicious sensation of fullness that left her breathless, wanting, completed. He wrapped himself around her and leaned his cheek against hers. "So good, Makenna. Every time is so fucking good."

Buried deep inside her, he devoured her mouth in a molten-hot kiss, and then he pulled free but held his face just above hers. His hips rocked and thrust and ground, picking up speed and demanding that she take more of him, all of him. He stole her breath and her ability to think and her heart until there was nothing left of her that he didn't own. Utterly and completely.

The depth of her emotions pricked at the backs of her eyes and made it so that all she could do was grasp his back and hold tight as his hips flew against hers. Because it was so much better than good.

How was it possible they'd only known each other for two months?

They'd met after spending a night trapped in a pitch-black elevator together, and their bond had been fast and deep—built on conversation that had revealed how much they had in common and a physical attraction that transcended appearances. If there'd ever been a silver lining around an otherwise bad situation, it had been having the freedom the darkness allowed to get to know him. And for him to get to know her. Since then, they'd been nearly inseparable.

Now, Makenna couldn't imagine her life without Caden Grayson.

And she hoped she'd never have to.

An hour later, Caden sat on the edge of the couch in Makenna's homey living room. His knee bounced. Tightness squeezed his chest. His teeth ached from how hard he was clenching his jaw.

What a fucking misfit.

Makenna was everything Caden was not—polished and out-going and able to put others at ease with her warm smile and her ready, open laughter. In the two months they'd been together, she'd totally embraced his friends and his interests and his world—inviting the guys at the firehouse over for dinner, cheering on his softball team, and even delivering a big tray of homemade brownies and chocolate chip cookies to the station. Hell, Makenna had all the guys there wrapped around her little finger at this point. And Caden was sure they looked at him and wondered how the hell he'd gotten so lucky.

Because he certainly wondered. Every damn day. And it made him sure it couldn't last. Or wouldn't. He couldn't be *that* lucky. At least, he'd never been before.

He shook his head and chuffed out a frustrated breath.

For the most part, he was a loner who was only comfortable around the guys he worked with and a small group of long-time friends. Over the last two months, Makenna had worked her way inside that small circle, after having broken down his walls and accepted all the bullshit she found behind them. He'd never been happier in his life. And he was having a damn hard time trusting it.

In his experience, happiness didn't last. Instead, it was ripped from you when you least expected, tearing you from the ones you loved and leaving you all alone. It was why he'd never before pursued a serious relationship with a woman. Until Makenna. Who was like a force of nature with her honesty and her positivity and her acceptance and her touch. He hadn't been able to resist the temptation of having something so good, something that might be able to shine some light on all his darkness.

"Okay, I'm ready," Makenna said, walking into the living room from the bedroom. She wore a beautiful smile and a lavender sweater over a pair of tight, sexy jeans tucked into knee-high brown leather boots. And, God, she was so damn pretty. Long, wavy red hair that he loved to play with swept across her face and settled around her shoulders. Her blue eyes were heaven in a stare, and saw right through all his masks. But instead of finding him unworthy— the way he felt—all that shined from those baby blues was affection and unconditional acceptance.

It slayed him. It really fucking did. Because she looked at him and never seemed to see all the defects he felt down deep.

"Great," Caden said, rising and swallowing the sour taste in the back of his throat. On the one hand, he wanted to meet her family. They were important to her, and so far in their relationship, he hadn't done nearly enough to meet her friends and get to know those she cared for the most. He owed this to her, and he wanted to be man enough—just once—to walk into a roomful of strangers and act like a normal freaking human being.

On the other hand, Caden was the furthest thing from normal. New people made him nervous as shit and he sucked at small talk. He never knew what to say, so he'd either clam up or end up with a foot in his mouth. Either way, he came off like an anti-social asshole. Much as he loved his ink and his facial piercings for a whole bunch of reasons, he couldn't say he was unhappy with the fact that his appearance scared some people off. Because being alone was miles better than being rejected, left, or abandoned.

Been there, done that, got the blood-stained T-shirt. Thank you very much.

Makenna came right up to him and wrapped her arms around his waist. "You look very handsome, Mr. Grayson." Her smile warmed his chest, and damn if her touch didn't make it easier to breathe. It had been like that from the start with Makenna—her presence easing his anxiety. He'd never had that with another person. He'd never even thought it was possible. "I hope you're not wearing long sleeves to cover your tattoos."

He was, though his dragon tattoo extended onto the back of his right hand, so there was only so much he could do about that. And they'd already had the conversation about his piercings—Makenna didn't want him to take them out for the visit, though he'd offered. "Just wanted to look nice."

Still holding one of his hands, she stepped back and gave him a long, slow once-over. Her gaze raked over his black dress pants and charcoal gray button-down shirt, a few of the nicer pieces he owned. A jeans-and-T-shirt kinda guy who worked in a uniform, Caden didn't have much use for dress clothes.

"So nice I'm tempted to take all this back off again." Her smile was pure temptation. "But seriously, I want you to be comfortable. Okay?"

Releasing a breath, he unbuttoned a sleeve and rolled it up. Repeated it on the other arm, revealing the whole dragon. Better already. On a roll, he undid another button at the collar. So much better. "There." He gave her a questioning smile.

"Perfection. And don't worry. They're going to love you. I promise."

He couldn't keep his eyebrow from arching. Highly fucking unlikely. "If you say so, Red." He tucked a silky wave behind her ear. Makenna's hair had been the very first thing he'd noticed about her.

Grinning, she nodded. "I do. Besides, with you being a paramedic and Patrick being a cop, I think you'll have lots in common to talk about. All of them love stupid humor movies, too. So it'll be just like us hanging out. Except with more penises." Pushing up on tiptoes, she pressed her body against him and hugged him tight.

Chuckling, Caden breathed her in, and her scent made his shoulders relax and his heart rate slow. *Get it together, Grayson. She needs this.* "Then let's do it," he said, forcing as much enthusiasm into his voice as he could.

"Yay," she said, with a radiant smile. "This is going to be great."

Nodding, Caden collected their bags and slung them over his shoulder as Makenna grabbed some things from the fridge. Maybe he could treat this weekend just like he did a run in the ambulance. When a call came in, Caden was able to focus on the crisis at hand in a way that blocked all the other shit out. In those moments, all that mattered was the person in need and what he could do to ease their pain and save their life. Just like someone had once done for him.

Surely he could focus, hold himself together, and do this for Makenna. "Of course it's gonna be great," he said, "because I'll be with you."

CHAPTER TWO

"So tell me about some of the weird calls you've responded to," Makenna said, smiling over at Caden. God, he was sexy sitting in the driver's seat of his black Jeep, big hands gripping the leather steering wheel. Though they were going home to visit her family, he was driving—he found her car, a little silver Prius, more confining than he could stand. They were halfway between her home in Arlington and her dad's place in Philadelphia and, as always, they never had trouble finding things to talk about. Heck, that was part of what drew her to Caden in the first place.

"There have been more than a few weird ones over the years," Caden said, quirking a small grin as he looked her way. "Let's see. There was the woman who got her hand stuck in the garbage disposal. Her sweater snagged on part of the internal mechanism. The sweater was cashmere and she was really pissed that we had to cut it."

Makenna grimaced. "Why'd she put her hand in the garbage disposal?"

"Dropped a ring down the drain," he said with a shrug of his broad shoulders. "We found it for her though." He pursed his lips and his eyes narrowed. "Oh. And once we got a call that a woman was hearing a man yell and scream through her apartment wall. We showed up with the police ten minutes later and he was fine. Turned out he'd been, uh, severely constipated and having a hard time...going."

Makenna burst out laughing. "That is gross. He must've been so embarrassed."

Caden chuckled. "I don't know. I think the woman who made the call was more embarrassed than he was. When we got there, she came out into the hallway with us because she was so worried about the guy."

"That's a big old case of TMI," Makenna said, enjoying the conversation. Being an EMT meant Caden confronted a lot of intense and often tragic situations, things about which he didn't always want to talk when he came home after a shift. So it was nice to learn more about this part of him.

Grinning so big it brought his dimples out to play, Caden nodded. Makenna loved how smiling made his face look so much younger and more relaxed. Between his head scar, the widow's peak of his shaved hair, and the piercings on his lip and eyebrow, his face could appear harsh, maybe even intimidating. Except when he smiled. "Then there was the guy who called because he thought his penis was going to explode. It turned out he'd borrowed Viagra without a prescription and taken three of them at once. Four days later, he still had an erection."

"Aw, God. What is wrong with people?" Makenna laughed and turned in her seat toward Caden.

"I don't know." Caden winked. "You'd be surprised how many strange calls we get. And dispatch gets the weirdest calls of all. People call to complain about fast food restaurants not getting their orders right, or to ask if the police could go to a movie theater and hold the show time up because they're caught in traffic, or to find out what the weather is. One old man called because he thought his house had suddenly started having a heartbeat. It turned out his new neighbors next door were in a band and he was hearing the drums. Oh, and then there was the old lady who called because her 72-year-old husband wanted to spice up their sex life by having a threesome. She wanted him arrested."

"Wow." Makenna shook her head. "I think I've called 9-1-1 exactly one time in my life, and it was when someone on the Metro thought they were having a heart attack. Even then I was nervous to dial the numbers."

"Well, that's how it should be," Caden said. "So many calls to 9-1-1- aren't emergencies at all."

Makenna reached over and laced her fingers with Caden's. Their clasped hands rested on his thigh, giving her a view of the dragon tattooed on the back of his right hand. "Okay, now tell me about some really great calls you went on."

"I've delivered three babies," he said, a small smile on his lips. "Those were my favorites. Such an amazing thing to be a part of, watching a life come into the world. You know? One of the couples named their son Grayson."

Her mouth dropped open. "Aw, Caden. That's so special. I can't imagine how scary it would be to know a baby was coming and not be able to get to the hospital." For a moment, Makenna's imagination ran away with the picture of this muscled, inked, pierced, scarred man holding a brand new baby in those big hands. What a sight that would be. She smiled.

"It was," he said with a nod. "I've also patched up a number of cats and dogs over the years, mostly pets that get trapped in house fires. Just to stabilize them until they get to a vet. But the people always appreciate it."

"Oh, be still my heart," Makenna said, squeezing his hand. "If I didn't already...like you, you would've totally won me over with your stories about babies and puppies." She looked out the windshield to the sunny blue sky beyond and hoped he didn't hear the way she'd tripped over her words. She'd nearly said she loved him. Because the feeling was always in the forefront of her mind these days.

He threw her a wicked grin. "How do you think Bear picks up so many different girls?" Isaac Barrett was a firefighter at Caden's station, and he was maybe the biggest player she'd ever met. But he was an also sweet and funny and loyal and would give a person the shirt off his back, and Makenna really liked him.

"Ah, so that explains it," she said.

"Pretty much." He lifted their joined hands to his mouth and pressed a kiss against her knuckles.

Heat lanced through Makenna's chest and her blood in equal measure.

Still holding hands, they settled into a comfortable silence. Makenna's gaze traced over what she could see of Caden's dragon tattoo, the one he'd gotten to remind himself not to let fear rule his life. She really admired the meaning behind many of his pieces, so much so that she'd been thinking of getting a tattoo herself. A lot. The idea whipped butterflies through her belly. She'd always been such a good-girl rule-follower that she'd never considered it seriously before meeting Caden. But, inspired by how he'd commemorated those he'd loved and lost on his skin, Makenna had been mulling over a few designs over the past couple of weeks.

I want to do this. The thought came firm and sure, and she felt the rightness of it down deep. "So, guess what I've been thinking about lately?"

"What's that?" he asked, his pierced eyebrow arching as he peered over at her.

It made her want to flick at his little black barbell piercing with her tongue. Her stomach flip-flopped as she gave voice to the idea. "Getting a tattoo."

Caden's gaze whipped toward her, his eyebrows cranked down over dark eyes. "For real?"

She grinned and bit her lip. "Yeah. I love yours and the more I think about it, the more I want to do it."

"What kind do you want?" he asked, his gaze dragging over her so hotly it almost felt like a physical caress.

"I've been thinking about a Celtic family tree. The one I like best is shaped like a circle and the tree and ground are made of Celtic knots. Some designs of it place initials below the ground or weave them into the branches, and that's really cool, too. Here," she said, dragging her finger against the screen of her smartphone. She opened an image she'd saved in her pictures and held it up so Caden could see. "This is one version of it."

His eyes flickered back and forth between her phone and the road ahead. "I like that," he said in a reserved tone. "A lot. How sure are you that you want to do this?"

"Pretty sure," she said. "I've been thinking about it a lot lately. It was just a matter of what to get. I wanted it to mean something, like yours do. So I thought about what means the most to me in the world, and it's family. Once I figured that out and found these designs, I was finally sure. But will you come with me if I get it done?"

He threw a blazing glance at her. "If you want to do this, I'd like to take you to my guy. He's the best there is. And of course I'll be there. In a heartbeat, Red."

She grinned and nodded. His presence would help steady her nerves. "Good," she said. "Maybe next week?"

"You just say the word," he said. "And I'll make it happen."

Makenna unbuckled her seat belt, stretched across the center console, and lingeringly kissed Caden's cheek, jaw, neck, letting her tongue sneak out to taste him while she was at it. He smelled good, like soap and mint and something spicy that was pure Caden.

He groaned and leaned into her touch. "Fuck, Makenna," he whispered. "I don't want you to stop but I really want you to put your seat belt back on."

She gave his ear lobe a final lick and settled back on her own side. "Sorry," she said as the buckle clicked. "I was just feeling really grateful."

He gave a little chuckle. "Well, I'll definitely take a raincheck on that. Besides, you can't put pictures in my head of you getting inked and then kiss on me like that while I'm driving."

"Why not?" she asked, biting on her lip to try to restrain the smile that threatened. And holy crap if the tone of his voice didn't make her wish he *wasn't* driving. Because she could think of some other very good uses for his hands....

The look he threw her—all blatant desire and frustration—shot heat over her skin. "Because it drives me crazy. And I can't do anything about it." He shifted his hips in the seat, drawing Makenna's gaze downward to the bulge forming in the front of his dress pants.

Slowly, she ran her hand down his chest and stomach to his lap.

"*Red,*" he rasped, his gaze drifting down to watch her hand rub and grip for just a moment. God, he was a delicious handful. Eyes back on the road, Caden shook his head and grabbed her hand, holding it in a ball against his chest. "I'm not chancing wrecking with you in the car." He threw her another one of those red-hot glances. "But you better believe we're revisiting this later."

Caden knew what Makenna was doing. For the past two and a half hours, she'd kept him talking non-stop. About his work. About tattoos. About Christmas. She'd teased him and made him laugh and generally kept his mind off of where they were going and what he was about to do—namely, meet her family. Which, of course, meant that she realized how anxious he was. And wasn't that a complete pisser.

Both because he didn't want her having to worry about such a thing and because she was right.

Following her directions, he veered off the highway into a suburb just south of Philadelphia.

"It's less than fifteen minutes from here," she said, excitement plain in her voice.

Caden nodded and tried like hell to ignore the tensing of his shoulders, the clenching of his gut, and the tightening of his chest. And man how he hated just how familiar these reactions were. Since the accident that had killed half of his family and left him alone with a bitter, angry, broken shell of a father at fourteen, Caden's body had always responded to stress this way. Working with a therapist years ago, he'd conquered the worst of his PTSD and anxiety and he had some techniques for battling the latter when it hit, but he couldn't stop it from happening or make it go away altogether.

Caden could never just be normal.

Something he could tolerate when it just impacted himself, but he hated it for Makenna's sake.

Holding the steering wheel in something close to a death grip, he silently counted backwards from ten, trying to remember his breathing techniques, trying to keep from freaking the fuck out before they even arrived. The last thing he wanted to do was embarrass Makenna in front of her family. Or embarrass himself.

It was vitally important that they like him—that they *accept* him—too.

Because Caden was falling for Makenna. Hard. Hell, he'd already loved her at least a little that first night they'd spent together. She'd kept him from having a full-on panic attack while trapped in that dark elevator, which had represented pretty much every one of his worst nightmares. And when she'd invited him in—to her home, to her bed, to her body for the first full night he'd ever spent in another person's arms, he'd probably already fallen most of the rest of the way.

Now, after two months of being with her, after two months of not being alone in every way a person could be alone—because of her, Caden felt like he stood on the edge of a tall cliff. One more step and he'd be free-falling head-first into a precipice from which he'd never return.

And it scared the ever-living fuck out of him.

Because he knew all too well how quickly and unexpectedly those he cared for the most could be torn from him. In the blink of a goddamned eye. And he'd have absolutely no say in it whatsoever. He wouldn't even see tragedy and heartbreak coming. Just like when he'd been fourteen.

Christ, Grayson. You're not helping things right now.

He heaved a deep breath and forced his fingers to loosen around the wheel. No, thinking about losing Makenna wasn't helping his state of mind at all.

"Hey," she said, squeezing his thigh. "Thank you for coming home with me."

The smile she gave him was so soft and pretty. It took the edge off of some of the anxiety building inside him. He could do this. He *would* do this. For her.

"You're welcome. I appreciate you inviting me." And he did. Despite all the churn in his head, it meant a lot that she'd wanted to be with him at Thanksgiving. It was nice not to be alone for once on a holiday. Hell, it was nice to be celebrating at all. His mom had always been the life of his family, and when she died, what was left of the Grayson family really died with her.

After she was gone, Caden's house never saw another Christmas tree, never baked another turkey, and never had another Easter basket waiting on the dining room table on Easter morning. Even after he and Sean had been way too old for baskets and Santa, she'd still marked presents "from Santa" and filled baskets that she insisted the Easter Bunny had delivered.

So being included in Makenna's family Thanksgiving celebration meant more than he could say.

Soon, Makenna was guiding them into a stately neighborhood full of big, older homes and manicured lawns and tall, mature trees. Most of the houses were made of gray limestone and sat back off the narrow streets, allowing room for wide covered porches and winter-bare gardens out front. Christmas wreaths and garlands of pine boughs and holly already adorned the doors and windows of some of the houses, making the neighborhood even more picturesque.

All of a sudden, curiosity replaced some of the anxiety flowing through Caden's body. Because all of this represented a part of Makenna he didn't know. He'd heard her talk about her father and brothers, of course, and he knew her mother died when Makenna was little, but hearing stories and actually *seeing* where she was from were two different things.

"My house is up here on the corner. Turn right, the driveway's on the side," Makenna said.

Caden rolled to a stop in front of the house and leaned to peer out Makenna's side window. Made of gray limestone, the place was beautiful. Three stories with a porch made for rocking chairs, windows flanked by black shutters, and soaring stone chimneys. An

American flag fluttered in the cold breeze from its perch on one of the gray porch columns. "This is where you grew up?" he asked.

"Yep," she said, smiling at him.

He met her gaze, and loved the happiness he saw there. Well, he loved so much more than that, didn't he? Even if he hadn't looked at that reality too closely. "It's really nice."

She looked out her window. "It was a wonderful place to grow up. Just being here gives me the warm and fuzzies."

Be-beep.

Caden's gaze flew to the rear-view and found a car sitting behind him. "Oh, shit, sorry," he said, making the right turn.

Makenna chuckled. "Don't worry about it. Oh, just park on the street," she said when they saw that four cars already took up most of the driveway in front of the two-car garage.

Caden pulled the Jeep to the curb and killed the engine.

"Looks like my brothers are all here, but I don't know who the Beemer belongs to," she said, shrugging. When she turned toward him, she was wearing a smile so full of excitement and anticipation that he was surprised she was managing to sit still. "Ready to meet everyone?"

At that moment, he wanted nothing more than to make her happy, so he nodded. "Ready as I'll ever be."

Now he just hoped he didn't fuck everything up.

CHAPTER THREE

"I'm home!" Makenna called as she pushed through the back door into the rectangular mud room. A big bench seat with hooks took up one wall, and Makenna placed the jug of apple pie sangria and the tray of pumpkin roll on the bench as she hung her coat. Caden settled their bags on the floor and did the same. The house smelled like roasting turkey and savory stuffing and cinnamon, and it was so welcoming that her heart squeezed for the want of seeing her dad and brothers.

Her father rushed into the doorway that led to the kitchen. "There's my peanut."

Makenna laughed. "Dad," she said as they hugged. She didn't mind the ancient nickname. Not really. And, oh, it was good to see him. She stood back from the hug and took him in—his brown hair had a bit more gray in it since she'd last seen him over the summer, but otherwise he looked exactly the same. Bright blue eyes. Laugh lines from a lifetime of good humor. And wearing the old apron with a picture of a turkey breast and the words *I'm a breast man!* her brothers had thought was a hilarious gift at least ten years before. "I want you to meet Caden," she said, stepping aside to let the men shake.

"Caden Grayson, sir," he said as he shook her father's hand. She could hear the nerves in his voice, but she had absolutely no doubt about her father's ability to put Caden at ease. "Happy Thanksgiving."

"You, too. Call me Mike." Her dad clasped Caden's shoulder and guided him into the kitchen. "What can I get you to drink?" he asked, then rattled off a long list of choices.

"A Coke would be fine," Caden said, standing beside the big island in the center of the open, airy kitchen.

Makenna brought her contributions to dinner in and sat them on the counter. The rustic white cabinets, honey-colored granite counters, and warm wooden floors had always made this her favorite room in the house. But man, if she didn't like the room even better with Caden there. "I'll get it," Makenna said, grinning to herself as she leaned into the fridge. Everything was better with Caden.

Her dad engaged them in small talk about the traffic and the nice weather they were having and how much longer the turkey still had to cook, and Makenna could see the tension draining out of Caden's shoulder. She covered his hand with hers where it rested against the countertop.

Her dad took casual notice of the gesture but otherwise didn't react. Though she'd told her father all about Caden, she'd never brought a man home before, so it was new ground for both of them. "So, Caden, Makenna tells me you're a paramedic. What's that like?"

"It's…" Caden's brow furrowed for a long moment. "It's different every day depending on the calls we get. Sometimes it's long hours of hanging out at the station, but most days you can hardly catch your breath for running between calls. Depending on how critical the situation is, it can be hard and stressful, but mostly it's an amazing privilege to be there to help someone in a moment when they desperately need it."

Makenna's heart swelled at the passion in his voice. Despite all he'd been through—not just the accident and the loss of his mom and brother, but the life-long PTSD and having a father who hadn't been there for him, too—Caden was such a sweet, good man. Two months ago, he'd held the elevator door for her when nothing else in her day had gone right, and she'd called him her Good Samaritan. Then, she hadn't known the half of it.

Her father nodded as he pulled a big dish down from a cabinet, and Makenna could see that the thoughtfulness of Caden's response had impressed him. "I have a lot of respect for first responders. You're out there on the front lines."

"When you've had a stranger show up to help you during your darkest hour, the least you can do is be there for someone else during theirs," Caden said in a quiet voice. "I've always felt that I had to pay it forward."

Makenna slipped her arm around Caden's waist. Part of her couldn't believe he'd offered that up, because she knew he didn't like to talk about himself. And it made her so proud of him that it took everything she had not to pull his face down for a kiss. But maybe it was better not to freak her father out fifteen minutes after arriving.

"Makenna told me about the accident," her dad said, taking a drink from a bottle of beer. "I was sorry to hear it. That's a lot for a kid to go through. But I'd say you're doing your family proud."

Caden gave a tight nod and looked down, suddenly very interested in his can of Coke.

She squeezed him tighter, because her dad was right. But Makenna changed the topic because she knew the attention—and the compliment—probably made him uncomfortable. "Where are the guys?" she asked, moving to fill a glass with sangria. Full of apples, cinnamon, and spice, it was fall in a cup. Delicious.

"Downstairs in the rec room," her dad said, peering into the oven to check the turkey. "Watching football, I think."

After her mother had died of breast cancer when Makenna was three, her dad took over everything her mother used to do—including the cooking. And he was good at it, too. Not that she remembered much of her mother. Of any of them, Patrick had the most memories because he'd been ten when they lost her. But even his memories were mostly faint and indistinct. Which explained why she and her brothers worshipped her dad. He'd been everything to them.

"Oh, and you're not the only one who brought a date home." Dad grinned, loving knowing something she didn't.

"Who else brought someone?" she asked. Patrick was married to the police department, so she knew it wasn't him, and she hadn't heard about Ian or Collin dating anyone. What the heck?

"Wanna guess?" her father asked as he pulled two cookie sheets of appetizers out of the second oven. He settled them on the counter.

"No!" Makenna said. "Spill already."

Her dad smiled and scooped the southwest egg rolls, pigs in a blanket, and spinach-artichoke pockets onto a platter. "Collin."

Her little brother brought a date? Holy crap. "Someone from grad school?" Makenna asked.

Her dad nodded. "Shima. She's a real sweetheart. You should go make sure she's surviving your brothers and introduce Caden." He took a cautious bite of one of the egg rolls. "And take these down for me?" he asked, tapping the edge of the dish.

Makenna grabbed a stack of paper plates and napkins. "Did you know she was coming?"

"Nope. It was a surprise." Her dad shrugged. "The more the merrier at the holidays, though."

Nodding, Makenna reached for the appetizers.

"I got it," Caden said.

"Great to meet you, Caden," her dad said. *"Mi casa es su casa.* So while you're here, make yourself completely at home." Makenna gave her dad a grateful smile for welcoming Caden, not that she'd doubted he would.

"Appreciate that, Mike," Caden said, following Makenna across the room and into a hallway.

At the top of the basement steps, she turned to him, smiling. "Just remember, I am in no way responsible for the cretins you're about to meet."

⌒⌒⌒⌒⌒

"Duly noted," Caden said, giving her a wink. If they were anything like Mike, he might actually make it through this weekend. He followed her down the steps.

The basement family room was a big, comfortable space with overstuffed sofas and chairs grouped in front of a large flat-screen television. At the far end sat an old air hockey table. But he didn't have time to take much more in before five pair of eyes settled on them.

"Hey," Makenna said to a big round of greetings. Her brothers— clear from the various shades of red hair—all got up to give her a hug. Which left a fourth guy with blond hair and Ken-doll good looks who Caden didn't know. Makenna took the tray of appetizers from Caden's hands as she said, "Uh, guys, this is Caden Grayson." She introduced her brothers, but seemed suddenly nervous.

"I'm Patrick," the first brother said, holding out his hand. He was the oldest James brother—seven years older than Makenna if Caden remembered right. Tall with reddish-brown hair and a close-trimmed beard, he wore a friendly smile as they shook.

"Nice to meet you, Patrick. I've heard a lot about you," Caden said.

"I'm Ian," the next brother said, his expression not as friendly. He stepped back from their handshake fairly quickly and fell into conversation with the mystery blond man—who Makenna was staring at, a frown on her face.

The last brother had the brightest red hair, so red it was almost orange. "Caden, I'm Collin and this is my girlfriend Shima," he said with a friendly, open smile. Caden shook both of their hands.

Shima pushed her sleek black hair over her shoulder and smiled conspiratorially. "We can stick together today if the James clan decides to gang up on the newcomers."

Caden chuckled. "You've got a deal."

"Dad made some appetizers," Makenna said, holding it out to everyone before settling the tray on the coffee table. "So, Cameron, hey. Wow. How long has it been?"

The blond-haired man stepped up to her with a smile Caden didn't really like. An interested smile. Who was this guy and why did Makenna seem unhappy to see him? "Too long, Makenna. You look great." He gave her a big, long hug. When the guy finally let her go, he tugged playfully—familiarly—at the end of a strand of her hair. "You haven't changed a bit."

With a chuckle, Makenna stepped back. "Oh, I don't know about that." She held her hand out to Caden. "Cam, this is Caden Grayson."

Cameron gave him a quick, assessing look that immediately set Caden's teeth on edge. They shook in a quick perfunctory greeting, and Caden couldn't help but wonder why it had just gotten so frosty.

Standing with Ian at his side, Cameron asked, "So what do you do, Caden?"

"I'm a paramedic," Caden said. "You?"

"I'm a cardiology fellow at Penn," he said.

"That's impressive," Caden said, taking a drink from his can of Coke. A doctor. And not just any doctor, but a specialist. Of course he was.

"Thanks. You have any interest in medical school?" Cameron asked.

"Nope," Caden said. "Emergency medical services is exactly where I always wanted to be." Which was the truth. When he was younger, he'd thought about pursuing a medical degree for about five seconds, but what he most wanted was to be there for people in crisis the way someone had once been there for him—out on the streets where things were messy and situations were still evolving and pre-hospital treatment was the difference between life and death. Plus, he hadn't wanted to spend all those years in school. He didn't have the patience for it.

"Huh," Cameron said with a shrug. "Well, good for you." His response plucked at Caden's last good nerve. Why did the guy make him feel like there was some competition he didn't know he was competing in?

Patrick joined their group. "You're in Arlington, is that right?"

Caden nodded, glad for the break from Cameron. "Yeah."

"Any chance you know Tony Anselmi? Arlington County police. I went to high school with him," Patrick said.

"Yeah," Caden said with a smile. "Our paths cross. I last saw him probably three weeks ago." As he and Patrick fell into a conversation about Tony and their respective jobs, Caden kept half his attention on the conversation between Makenna, Cameron, and Ian.

"You still crunching numbers?" Cameron asked her, his tone borderline condescending. Or maybe it only sounded patronizing because the guy rubbed Caden the wrong way. Caden frowned, knowing Makenna loved her job as a forensic accountant.

"Yup," Makenna said. "You still playing with people's hearts?"

Cameron burst out laughing.

"Geez, Makenna," Ian said.

"What? He's a cardiologist," she said.

"It's all good, it's all good," Cameron said. He tilted his beer bottle toward her as if in salute. "Touché."

Smiling, Makenna shook her head and sipped at her sangria.

Soon, they all settled onto the couches and chairs to watch football, which had never really been Caden's thing, though he didn't mind watching. Patrick sat in one of the big leather armchairs, and Ian, Collin, and Shima took one of the couches. That left him, Makenna, and Cameron for the other couch. She sat down first, which put him and Cameron on either side of her. Fantastic.

"So, how long have you two been dating?" Ian asked.

Makenna put her hand on Caden's thigh, and he appreciated the hell out of the claiming gesture. "A little over two months," she said, giving Caden a smile. Over her shoulder, he saw Cameron and Ian exchange a look. What the hell? Was he imagining this shit? Who was the guy, anyway?

"How about you two?" Makenna said, looking at Collin and Shima. "How long have you been dating?

The couple exchanged smiles, and then Collin said, "Since the end of the summer. We've known each other since we both started the Master's program, but got together at the welcome-back party in August."

"It's good when grad students date other grad students," Shima said. "Because then we don't bore other people silly with all our foreign policy shop talk."

Caden smiled. He liked Shima and was really glad she was there. "So, Ian, Makenna told me you're an engineer. What kinds of things do you work on?" he asked, hoping to get the middle James brother to warm up to him.

"I'm a civil engineer for the city of Philadelphia," he said. "I focus primarily on road, bridge, and tunnel projects."

"So it's all *your* fault," Patrick said with a grin.

Ian flipped him the finger as everyone laughed.

"Seriously," Patrick said, holding a hand out to Caden. "Have you driven around Philly much?" Caden shook his head. As a kid, his family used to roadtrip everywhere, but since the accident, Caden hadn't traveled much out of the DC area. "Well, trust me, driving in Philly sucks. I would know since I do it every day."

"Yeah, yeah, yeah," Ian said, glaring at his brother. "Same shit, different day."

"Cameron," Shima said, "what's your connection to the Jameses?" Caden wanted to high five her for asking.

"This knucklehead's my best friend," Cameron said, pointing at Ian. "Has been since grade school." Pause. "And Makenna and I dated for what?" He looked at her with a smile. "Three years?"

Dated? Three years? Caden looked at Cameron, who was wearing a satisfied expression that said he knew Caden hadn't known about their past. And he was right.

"Uh, yeah," Makenna said. "Three years."

Three years. Caden had never dated *anyone* for three years. Hell, Caden had rarely dated at all before Makenna. He took a long drink of his soda.

"We started dating my senior and her sophomore year of college," he said. Makenna just nodded. Caden ran the mental calculations. She would've been about nineteen when they started dating and twenty-two when they broke things off. Which pretty much meant there was no way in hell they hadn't slept together. *Whiiich* explained the way the guy had been looking and smiling at her, and how he'd hugged her longer than necessary. He was still into her.

"God, that seems like a million years ago," Makenna said with a smile. She took a long drink of her sangria.

"Nah," Cameron said with a wink. "Hey, do you remember that time when we—"

"Can I get some help setting the table?" came Mike's voice down the stairs.

"I'll help," Makenna called, grasping Caden's hand. "Wanna join me?"

"Yeah," he said. She could've asked him if he wanted to help her clean toilets with toothbrushes and he would've agreed. Anything to take a break from Cameron's smug face, and from the way the man's eyes followed Makenna's body as she rose from the couch.

CHAPTER FOUR

Upstairs, Makenna dragged Caden into the hall bathroom and shut the door. "I didn't know he was going to be here," she said. From the moment she'd looked up and seen Cameron Hollander standing there, she'd worried about Caden's reaction. Why hadn't Dad warned her? Although, she wasn't sure what she could've done even if she'd known.

"Okay," he said, and then he shrugged. His expression seemed unconcerned, but she knew he was capable of throwing down a shutter over his true feelings when he didn't want to confront them. Hell, separating himself from his emotions had been half of how he'd survived the aftermath of losing his family, so he was damn near an expert at it. "It's fine."

She dropped her forehead against his chest, wrapped her arms around his waist, and breathed him in. "It's awkward."

Caden chuckled as he stroked the back of her hair. "Only because he's still interested."

Groaning, Makenna shook her head, totally confused by Cam's presence and annoyed that it might make Caden uncomfortable. Finally, she lifted her gaze to meet Caden's. "Well I'm not interested in him, in case that needs to be said." It had been three years since they parted ways, and she'd been over Cam for a long time. He'd made his choice and she'd made her peace with it.

Caden's dark gaze studied her for a moment. He gave a small shake. "It doesn't, Makenna. Don't worry. Although if he stares at your ass or plays with your hair one more time, I won't be held accountable for my actions." The pierced eyebrow arched playfully.

She chuckled, but God, she really didn't want anything to mess up this visit or make Caden feel any more uncomfortable than she knew he already did. She was going to kill Ian, who knew that Makenna was bringing someone home. What the hell had he been thinking? "Would you like to know the story—"

The door handle jiggled.

"Someone's in here," she called.

"Okay," came Ian's voice.

"Let's go help with the table," Caden said. "We can talk later."

She nodded, and thrilled when he bent down and gave her a long, slow, wet kiss full of heat and passion and tongue. From the first time they'd kissed in the darkness of that elevator, his kissing skills had totally owned her. "I'm sorry, what were you saying?" she asked in a breathy voice when he pulled away.

The smile he gave her brought out his dimples. "I don't know, but you taste like apples and cinnamon."

"It's my sangria. You should try some."

"I think I will." His big hand slipped behind her neck as he kissed her again. A deep, exploring kiss. "Mmm, that's good," he rasped.

"God, I could kiss you like that all day," she whispered.

His grin was full of smug masculine satisfaction. "Could you now?" With a wink, he turned and opened the door.

Down the hall, they ran into Ian. "Were you seriously in the bathroom together?" he asked.

Makenna glared, not appreciating his standoffishness toward Caden downstairs. "Did you seriously bring my ex-boyfriend to Thanksgiving?"

"He's my best friend," Ian said, stepping past them. True, but it had been a lot of years since Cameron had celebrated a holiday with them. When they were all younger, it hadn't been unusual for Cameron to be at their house for meals and sleepovers, including the holidays. But he hadn't last been there since before she and Cam broke up.

When her brother closed himself in the bathroom, she turned to Caden. "Sorry about him. Not sure what his problem is."

On one level, she wasn't surprised that Ian was the one to cause trouble where Caden was concerned. Because Patrick was so much older, she'd always idolized him and he'd always been an awesome big brother to her—they always got along great. And because Collin was younger and generally the easiest-going person you'd ever meet, she usually didn't end up having issues with him. But her and Ian—the two middle kids—butted heads over just about everything and anything, and always had.

"Loyalty, I'm guessing." He kissed the top of her head. "Stop worrying."

"Okay," she said. They went into the kitchen to find her father pulling the turkey out of the oven. "How can we help?"

"Collin and Shima started on the table. See if they want help and, if not, you can start plating everything. We'll be ready to eat in about twenty minutes. Just need to make some gravy."

"Okay," Makenna said, leading Caden into the dining room that hosted every meal whenever the whole family got together. Collin and Shima were setting out plates and silverware around the big formal table.

"Wait. You forgot Mom's runner," Makenna said.

"Oh, shit," Collin said. "Sorry."

"It's no problem," Makenna said, going to the glass-fronted hutch that sat on the far wall. She found the decorative cloth in the bottom cabinet. "When my mom died, my dad was really good about sharing all the traditions that had been important to her. My grandmother made this and gave it to Mom as a present, and Mom apparently used it every Thanksgiving." She unfolded the long rectangle with embroidered leaves and pumpkins and acorns. "We still like to use it."

Caden helped her spread it out down the length of the table between the place settings Collin had already set out.

"It's beautiful," Shima said. "It's really special that you still honor her this way."

"Yeah," Makenna said. "Collin and I were too young to really remember much of her, so it's nice to have things like this." She shrugged. "I've always felt like, if I can't have her, I have to hang on to whatever parts of her I can have. I don't know."

Caden's arm fell around her shoulders and he hugged her against him. "Shima's right. It's a special thing to do." The sweetness of his words unleashed warmth in her chest. God, she loved this man.

They made quick work of setting the rest of the table and then Makenna and Caden returned to the kitchen to help with the rest of the food. One by one, Makenna filled serving dishes and platters and Caden took them out to the table for her.

She and Caden had made a million meals together over the past few months, but there was something really special about the two of them working on a meal in the house where she grew up. It made Caden feel like part of the family, because to her he already was. Finally, the turkey was carved and the gravy was ready, and it was time to eat. Her father called everyone to the table.

Her father and Patrick sat at the ends, and Collin, Shima, and Ian sat on the far side. Cam went for the middle seat on the close side, which would put him between her and Caden. Not happening.

"Hey, Cam? Would you mind moving down one so Caden and I can sit together?" she asked, perturbed that he'd *made* her ask. She wasn't sure what he was up to with this visit, but she wasn't playing, whatever it was.

"Sure," he said, sliding over.

"Here you go," Caden said, pulling out the end chair for her so he'd end up between them.

She hid her grin as she sat next to her father and Caden took the middle seat. Score one for Caden.

Her father held out his hands, and they all followed suit. Out of nowhere, sitting at Thanksgiving dinner holding the hands of the two most important men in her life made her throat tight with gratitude and joy. Dad bowed his head. "Thank you, God, for fulfilling all our needs and blessing us with this food. Thank you for each person who shares this meal with us today. May our lives never be so rushed and busy that we don't remember to stop and be grateful, to see all the things we have in this life. Our family, our friends, our homes, our health, our jobs. And may those who are less fortunate get everything they need this Thanksgiving, and may we always do our part to make their lives better. Amen."

"Amen," they all echoed.

Makenna smiled at Caden and gave his hand an extra squeeze before she let it go. The incredible serendipity of getting stuck in that elevator with him was the thing she was most grateful for right now, because she couldn't imagine her life without him. His quiet generosity, his selflessness, his protectiveness, his sarcasm, the adoring way he looked at her, the way their bodies fit together—there were so many things to love about him.

Soon their plates were piled high and everyone was digging in. Makenna was well into her second cup of sangria and the warmth of it was spreading through her.

"Everything's great, Mike," Caden said. A chorus of agreements rose up all around the table.

"Shima," Makenna said. "Where are you from?"

"I grew up in New York," she said, "though my mother is from Japan. She met an American sailor and fell in love and here I am."

Makenna smiled. She really liked this woman and was super excited for Collin. "That's so romantic. There really is something about a man in a uniform."

"Why, thank you," Patrick said.

Rolling her eyes, Makenna laughed. "I didn't exactly have you in mind." She winked at Caden, who gave her a crooked grin. Even though his wasn't as fancy as some, he looked damn sexy in his uniform—especially knowing he'd be helping people and saving lives while wearing it.

Patrick pointed his fork at Caden. "They just relaxed the tattoo policy in our department last year," he said. "Used to be you couldn't have any showing. Now you can have one showing on each arm. They give you any problems with that?"

Caden shook his head. "Arlington doesn't have any policy regarding tattoos. But most of mine are covered anyway."

"Your dragon's beautiful," Shima said. "I've always wanted a tattoo."

Makenna's belly did a little flip, and then she decided to share the news, because she'd have to at some point anyway. "I'm going to get one."

Things suddenly got quiet at the table.

"Really? What are you going to get?" Shima asked, not yet cluing into the fact that all the James men were looking at Makenna like she had three heads—and looking at Caden like he'd introduced her to drinking the blood of bats. No one in her family had any tattoos.

Makenna glanced at her father, whose expression was largely neutral, though probably carefully so. "A Celtic family tree with all our initials. I wanted a design that meant something to me. And nothing is more important to me than the people at this table." Her father's gaze softened. Annnd she won him over.

"Just give it a lot of thought," her dad said. "But your idea sounds great."

"Thanks," she said.

"Why do you want a tattoo?" Ian asked, an edge to his tone that said he thought he knew.

"Because I like them."

"Since when?" he asked.

She nailed him with a stare and debated throwing her corn bread at him. Except that would be a terrible waste of corn bread. They might be twenty-seven and twenty-five respectively, but they still had the ability to bring out the twelve-year-old in each other. "Since a long time. I just wasn't sure what I would want before."

"A lot of guys on the force have them," Patrick said. She could've hugged him for the show of support. "They're pretty mainstream these days."

"My father has quite a few," Shima said. "A lot of military stuff, as you might imagine. Initials of friends who died. Some of them are very moving, to see what he found important enough to memorialize on his body."

Makenna nodded. Caden's tattoos were the same way. He had a yellow rose on his chest for his mother, Sean's name and Chinese characters that meant "never forget" on his shoulders, and the dragon on his hand and arm which was his reminder to fight his fear so he could live when Sean couldn't, among others. The accident had truly marked him inside and out.

"I need more sangria. Can I get anyone something while I'm up?" Makenna asked.

"I'd love to try some," Shima said. Collin and her dad asked for some, too.

"I'll help you," Dad said, getting up.

She grabbed her glass and rose, and she gave Caden's shoulder a small squeeze before she stepped away. What she really wanted to do was kiss him, but she didn't want to make him uncomfortable by doing it in front of everybody.

In the kitchen, her dad grasped her arm. "Are you doing okay with Cameron being here? I didn't know Ian invited him until they showed up," he said in almost a whisper.

"It's fine," she said. "Ancient history, anyway." And it really was. She hadn't thought about Cameron in ages.

"I'm sorry I didn't say anything before you went downstairs. I didn't want to make you uncomfortable in front of Caden." He shook his head.

Makenna pressed onto tiptoes to kiss her father on the cheek. "Don't worry about it, Dad. Really."

They poured everyone's drinks and carried the out to the table.

"Need anything?" she asked, leaning closer to Caden.

He shook his head. "I have everything I need." The look he gave her said his words weren't about the food.

Conversation flowed around the table. About her Aunt Maggie, who'd been a mother figure to Makenna when she was a kid—she wasn't there this year because she'd gone on a cruise with a group of girlfriends. About Dad's painting, something he'd been doing for as long as Makenna could remember. About Cam's fellowship and where he hoped to land when it was done next year. About Collin and Shima's masters theses. And so much more. The conversation was lively and easy, and Makenna appreciated how much Caden joined in with this big group of people he didn't know. She knew that wasn't easy for him.

"Okay, everybody," her dad said. "Go unbutton your pants and rest your stomachs for a bit and I'll get this cleaned up and pull our dessert." Everyone laughed.

"We'll help, Dad. You did all the cooking," Makenna said.

"I won't protest that," he said with a grin.

Everyone pitched in on clearing the table. Patrick and Dad focused on boxing up all the leftovers, and Collin and Shima reset the table for dessert. Ian took out the overflowing kitchen trash.

"I'll rinse, you load?" Caden asked, stepping up to the sink. Makenna nodded with a smile. This was their routine at home, and she kinda adored that he didn't give a second thought to doing it here. "What?" he asked as he handed off a dirty.

She just smiled. "Nothing at all, Good Sam."

He rolled his eyes, but the look on his face was all contentment. Not something she saw all that often, and she totally adored it. "Hey look." He nodded toward the window.

"Oh, it's snowing," Makenna said. Just enough had come down to dust the tree branches and grass. It wasn't sticking to the roads yet, but even if it did, they were staying until Saturday. Snow was especially nice when you didn't have to drive in it. "How much are we supposed to get, Dad?"

"Just a couple inches. Enough to make it pretty." He gave her a wink.

"This was the nicest Thanksgiving I've had in a long time," Caden said, drying his hands once they'd finished. "Thank you for letting me be a part of it."

The sentiment melted Makenna's heart. She wanted him to enjoy himself so much. He had holiday meals at the fire station or occasionally with friends, but it had been a lot of years since Caden had celebrated a holiday with family. And given how tight her own was, that broke her heart. Everyone needed somewhere to belong, and she really wanted to be that for him. And her family, too.

Her father gave Caden a big smile. "I'm glad to hear it, Caden. But it's not over yet."

"Everything's all set," Collin said. "Sugar comas to commence in three, two, one."

"That is if the tryptophan doesn't set in first," Cam said.

"Either way, we'll all be asleep in an hour," Patrick said, clapping their dad on the back. They settled back around the dining room table, treated this time to a smorgasbord that included Makenna's pumpkin roll, a pumpkin pie, an apple pie, and a carrot cake that Shima made.

"I'm seriously going to need some of each," Makenna said.

"Oh, good. I was hoping I wouldn't be the only one," Caden said, taking a piece of her pumpkin roll. He passed her the plate.

The food went around and the conversation resumed, and even Ian seemed done with making little digs at her and Caden. So Makenna finally allowed herself to relax about the visit. Caden was doing great, just like she knew he would, and her family had taken him into the fold. Just like she told him. There'd been absolutely nothing to worry about.

CHAPTER FIVE

Standing in her childhood bedroom, Makenna shrugged into her favorite oversized sweatshirt, chilly after hours of watching movies with everyone in the basement. If Cameron hadn't been there, she would've just changed into pajamas given the late hour, but somehow it felt too familiar to do that given their history.

Why was he there? And what was he up to? All day, she'd felt him looking at her, watching her, trying to catch her eye. And all day, she'd pretty much ignored him and stuck by Caden's side, hoping to avoid giving Cam an in. Over the past few years, he'd texted or emailed her occasionally, and she heard stories about what he was up to from Ian when the family got together, but generally, they didn't have much contact anymore. Which was fine by her.

She tugged her boots off and ran a brush through her hair, then stepped out into the hall. When she rounded the bannister to go downstairs, her stomach dropped.

"Hey," Cam said, almost at the top of the steps.

"Hey," she said, waiting to go around him.

"Can we please talk for a minute?"

Alarm bells went off in her head. The final conversations they'd had several years ago hadn't been pleasant. Whatever this was, she wasn't looking forward to it. "I don't know."

"Come on, Makenna. Please?" He gave her *the look*, the one that once had melted her on sight.

She studied him for a moment—he had all-American good looks with blond hair, blue eyes, and a square jaw that was to die for, and wore a light gray V-neck cashmere sweater over a blue button down that made his eyes even brighter. Once, she'd thought there was no hotter man. And she'd been as attracted to his brain and his ambition as she was his looks. Not to mention his long association with her family, because she'd known Cam since her age ran in the single digits.

With a sigh, she nodded. "Okay. What do you want to talk about?"

He gestured toward her room. "Can we, maybe, talk somewhere more private?"

"I'd rather do it here," she said, crossing her arms. She was feeling a bit ambushed, which in turn made her irritated with both Cameron and Ian for setting it up. Because whatever it was he wanted to talk about was why he was here today. She knew that in her gut.

"Okay, then," Cameron said. "Well…the thing is…" He chuffed out a laugh. "I had this all planned, but now that you're standing in front of me, my tongue's all tied like I'm a teenager."

The self-deprecation was charming, as was the sheepish look on his face, but the sentiment set off more alarm bells.

He gave her a smile. "I miss you. That's the first thing I wanted to say. I miss you and I now know I made a huge mistake when I didn't take the fellowship in DC." Makenna's stomach flipped and the floor wobbled beneath her feet. "Actually, I knew it was a mistake almost immediately, but I was too immature and proud to admit it, and too scared to ask you to take me back."

No. Nonono. "Cam—"

"Please let me finish," he said with a tilt of his head. "I know I might not deserve it, but please?"

Heart racing fast, Makenna nodded. Even though she felt a little like she might throw up that second piece of apple pie she'd sneaked an hour ago. She didn't still have feelings for him, but that didn't make hearing this from someone she'd once loved any easier.

"I've done a lot of growing up and a lot of thinking about what I want in life. A prestigious match is still important to me, but not as important as having someone I care about to share my life with. I could've had that with you. I *should've* had that with you. And I still want it. With you," he said, his eyes blazing.

"Cameron, I'm with someone else now," she said, her insides all a-jumble at the surprise of this conversation. Never in a million years would she have expected this from him.

"I know," he said. "And I'm sorry for that. It's why I had to say something now, before you got serious with him. But you've only been dating for two months. We have a history that goes back twenty years. We were together for three of those. And we'd be married right now if I hadn't been a stubborn, selfish prick."

"I *am* serious with him," she said, the walls spinning around her. Once upon a time, she would've given everything to hear these words from him. But it was too late. She'd moved on. From

Cameron and with someone else. With Caden. "We've been apart for three years, too. A lot has changed."

Cam stepped closer. "How I feel about you hasn't changed. Or maybe it has. It's gotten stronger. I have a good lead on a position in DC when my fellowship ends. I want to try for that position and move down there. I want to be with you. I want us to start over and build the life together we should've already had."

"You're not listening—"

"I am. I hear you. You think you're serious about this guy. But he's the blink of an eye compared to how long we've known each other. If you gave us a chance—"

Makenna stepped back, away from his intensity, away from his touch, away from these words that tormented her only because they no longer mattered. And once they would've meant the world. There was a sadness in that that hurt. A lot.

He moved with her, staying close. "Please, give us a chance. Give *me* a chance." He pulled something from his pocket. A ring box. "I still have it," he said, cracking the velvet top open to reveal a stunning emerald-cut diamond in a magnificent setting. She remembered how beautiful it looked on her hand. "I would give anything to be able to earn my way back into your heart, to have the chance to hear you say again that you would marry me."

Swallowing around the knot in her throat, Makenna closed the ring box in his hands. "Cameron, I appreciate what you're saying. I do. But I moved on. You made your choice and I made mine. And *three years* have passed. Caden and I haven't been together very long, but that bears no relationship to how much I care about him. I can't turn that off, and I don't want to," she said. She didn't want to hurt Cameron's feelings, in fact she hated that her words might hurt him, but he'd waited too long. Damnit, that wasn't her fault.

Cam clasped his hands around hers. "Don't say no. Please. Just think about what I'm saying. I'll wait. I'll wait as long as you need to figure things out." Desperation shaped his classical features into a tortured mask she'd never before seen him wear, and it made her realize how sincere he was being just then. Which meant he really had grown up a lot since they'd split.

Her heart ached for what they might've been. "I don't think I need to think about it, Cam."

"I'll wait, Makenna. Because I love you," he gave a helpless shrug. "I've loved you so much of my life."

She'd said those words to him once, but now when she thought of love it was Caden's face that came to mind. Caden's touch. Caden's eyes. "Where were you three years ago, or even two?"

He shook his head. "So lost. Clearly. Just think about it, okay?"

Her shoulders sagged. She didn't want to fight with him. She didn't want to hurt him. And she didn't want to ruin Thanksgiving. What was she supposed to say? "Okay," Makenna blurted, already mentally drafting the email where she told him they were through, for good.

She inhaled to say more when Cameron suddenly stepped fully into her space and pressed his lips to hers. Makenna was so stunned it took her a moment to realize what had happened.

She wrenched back and glared. "*Don't.* You know what? I don't need to think about this. I meant what I said. I'm with Caden right now. I have no intention of stopping being with him because we've had this talk."

He held up his hands. "I'm sorry. I'm really sorry. I understand. I just…I just miss you."

"I need to get back downstairs now," Makenna said, and without another word, she slipped around him and padded down the steps.

And then she locked herself inside the hall bathroom, pressed her back against the door, and slapped her hand over her mouth. What the hell just happened?

"Okay," Makenna had said. And with just that one word, Caden's whole world tilted on its axis and sent everything reeling.

He bolted from where he'd been standing near the bottom of the steps, having gone looking for Makenna to see if she wanted anything before he made himself a turkey sandwich. And he'd overheard her entire conversation with Cameron. The guy missed her, loved her, and wanted her back—well, that much had been clear most of the day, hadn't it?

Bee-lining through the house, he was glad everyone else was still downstairs. He made for the kitchen, then the back door, then his Jeep, just for space, just to escape, just to find some place where there might still be some oxygen left to breathe. Outside, he braced his hands on the hood of the Jeep, not caring about the snow or the way the cold wetness of it immediately made his fingers ache.

As if all that wasn't bad enough, to learn that Makenna had once agreed to marry that guy. That they would've *already* been married if Cameron hadn't made some mistake. Caden hadn't gotten all the details, but they didn't really matter. What mattered was that Makenna had loved Cameron enough to want to make a life with him. A life with a man who was Caden's opposite in just about every way—professional where Caden was blue collar, wealthy where Caden was just comfortable, all-American good looks where Caden appeared rough around the edges, confident and charming where Caden was awkward and clumsy.

Cameron was the kind of guy Makenna was attracted to when she met a man in the light of day. The darkness in that elevator had been Caden's saving grace, because it had allowed both of them to get to know one another without the preconceptions that appearances created—and he'd created some of his on purpose, hadn't he? Except once he'd gotten to know her within the freedom of that darkness, he hadn't wanted her to turn him away when she saw him. He hadn't wanted her to be put off by him.

And, miraculously, she hadn't been. He could still hear her calling him *freaking gorgeous* that night. And the memory of it still stole his breath and set his heart to racing. But if Cameron was the kind of man she'd once agreed to marry, then it proved that her attraction to Caden was a fluke. At the very least, not her norm. Didn't it? Did that matter?

Maybe it didn't. Or at least shouldn't.

But it made him doubt, for maybe the millionth time since they'd started seeing one another, whether he was good enough for her, whether he was right for her. He thought he'd put the worst of that behind him, because he knew it was his past and his anxiety and his fucked-up fears talking. He knew it was. But seeing an alternative future for Makenna held up in front of his face like this had reached inside his chest and his brain and his heart and stirred it all up again.

Stirred it up bad.

Jesus.

Breathe, Grayson. Just fucking breathe.

He braced wet hands on his knees, lowered his head, and counted backward from ten. *Ten.* Deep in, deep out. *Nine.* Deep in, deep out.

Eight. If it hurt this bad to imagine Makenna with someone else, how much would it hurt to lose her? *Seven.* Deep, in, deep out. *Six.* I've lost everyone else, why would she be different? *Five.* Deep in, deep out. *Four.* You have her now, focus on that. *Three.* Okay, okay. *Two.* Deep in, deep out. *One.* Deep in, deep out.

Shit, his shoulders and chest were just as tight.

He did it again from ten, this time blocking out all the non-stop commentary racing through his head.

When he was done, he stood up and rolled his neck, his shoulders. She'd only agreed to think about what Cameron had said to her. She hadn't agreed to be with him and she'd made it clear that she was serious about Caden. *Focus on that.* Right. Okay.

Except hearing the echo of Cameron's declaration of love in his ear added another layer of stress to the whole situation. Because that dickhead had said it to Makenna again when Caden hadn't said it once yet.

In fact, the prospect of declaring how he felt scared the shit out of Caden. Because it felt like tempting the fates. *Hey, lightning, let me show you what I really care about so you know where to strike next!*

The past. Anxiety. Fucked-up fears. He knew it.

Didn't change that he felt that way though.

Which brought him back around to the gut check that maybe he wasn't good enough for her.

Because didn't Makenna deserve to hear those words? And if Caden couldn't give them to her ....

Then what?

Stop it. Get back in there and be with her. That's how you keep her.

He scrubbed his hand over the scar on his head. "Fuck," he bit out. And then he turned on his heel and got back in the house. He could pull himself together. *Nothing* had happened, nothing had changed. She'd show him.

"Hey, there you are," Makenna said, standing at the kitchen counter stirring a cup of hot tea. "I was looking for you."

"Just needed a little air," Caden said, joining her at the counter.

"Family proving a little too much?" she asked with a smile. She wrapped her arms around him. "Oh, you're so chilly. I better warm you up." Pressing herself tight against him, she held him closer and tucked her head in against his throat.

The embrace was fucking life.

He hugged her back. "Not too much," he said, clearing the roughness out of his voice. "I like your family. It's been a great day." And it was. He'd meant it when he told Mike he hadn't had a Thanksgiving this enjoyable in years.

"Would you like anything?" she asked.

His appetite for that turkey sandwich was long gone. "No," he said. "I'm good."

"Would you like to go be alone, just the two of us?"

He didn't even have to think. "That sounds like heaven," he said.

Makenna's smile was like the sun coming out from behind the clouds. *See how she's looking at you? Trust that look, Grayson. Nothing else matters.*

She grasped his hand. "Then come with me."

CHAPTER SIX

When they made it to her room, Makenna closed the door. "It's only a double bed, so I hope you're not too cramped tonight with me."

"We're sleeping together?" he asked, looking around her childhood room. Pieces of her youth remained tacked to the lavender walls and hung from her mirror. Ribbons, photographs, posters of bands. The room spoke of a person who grew up in the warm embrace of family, happiness, wholeness. "Your father doesn't mind?"

Chuckling, Makenna shook her head. "We practically live together, Caden, which he knows. I'm sure he's figured out that his twenty-five-year-old daughter has had sex before. Collin and Shima are sleeping together, too."

"Shima's pretty awesome," he said, wondering if Makenna would say anything to him about her conversation with Cameron.

"She really is," Makenna said with a smile. And then she unbuttoned her jeans, pushed them down, and took them off altogether, leaving her standing there in an oversized, faded red and blue Penn sweatshirt that was just long enough to cover her panties. "You should get undressed, too," she said, coming to him and starting on the buttons of his shirt.

Press and release, press and release. Until she was pulling his shirt from his dress pants and exposing his skin.

She gave a little moan and kissed the center of his chest. "Just like unwrapping a present." She trailed a line of kisses and licks from one nipple to the other.

"Fuck, Makenna," he whispered. "What are you doing?"

"Tasting you," she said.

The words were like a blowtorch to his blood. He was hard in an instant. "We can't," he said, though his hands went to the back of her head, encouraging her, guiding her as she continued to kiss and tease and drive him wild with her mouth.

"We can if we're quiet." Slowly, she dropped to her knees and bared him to mid-thigh. She took his cock in hand and gripped him firmly, tearing a soft grunt from his throat. "I've been wanting you all day," she whispered, her lips teasing his head with soft kisses.

"Wanting to touch you and kiss you and hold you. I can't hold back anymore." She licked him from root to tip. Once, twice, three times. And then she sucked him into her mouth.

It felt so fucking good that Caden's hands flew to her hair, digging in, grabbing hold. She moaned at the contact and pushed herself deeper, burying his cock in the back of her throat. The intensity of it nearly took his knees out from underneath of him.

Makenna pulled off his length. "Lay down on the floor."

He was too far gone to debate the wisdom of having sex in her father's house. He needed this. He needed *her*. He needed the connection and the coming together of the act. Caden locked the door, took the rest of his clothes off, and spread himself out on the beige carpet.

She undressed, too, all that beautiful red hair spilling around the bare porcelain of her shoulders and making him think of peaches and cream. And, *fuck*, he was starving.

Caden grasped his cock. "Take me back in your mouth."

He didn't have to ask twice. Makenna settled herself between his legs and wrapped her lips around his cock. She sucked him deep and slow, than fast and shallow, her baby blues flashing up at him so fucking sexy. He needed to see her eyes, so he fisted her hair into a ponytail to keep it out of her face. He used his grip to urge her harder, faster, deeper. He needed it. *God*, he needed it. And she took it. She took everything he gave her and so much more.

"Fuck, Red, I'm gonna come if you don't stop," he whispered.

She pulled off him, her lips shiny and swollen. "I want you inside me first," she said, already crawling up his body.

Caden reached for his pants and fished a condom out of his wallet. Rolled it on with shaking, needy hands. Then he gripped her hip. "Take all of me, Red. Fucking take all of me." The words came from someplace inside him that was raw and wounded and so full of yearning.

"Yes," she whispered, sinking down, impaling herself on him inch by maddening inch. "Oh, God, it's so good."

"Jesus," he rasped. Every urge inside him had him wanting to flip her over, to pin her down, to drive himself into her until they were both screaming and coming and losing their minds. But there was no way that would be quiet. He had to let her lead this. His hips surged when she'd taken him all the way. "Ride me, Makenna. Use me."

She planted her hands on his chest and lifted herself up and down his length, her slickness coating him and creating the most delicious friction. Their breaths were the only sounds in the room, and the way she gasped and pressed her lips together and furrowed her forehead proved she was having to work to be quiet. "Shit, Caden," she breathed.

Their gazes collided, hot and needy. He gripped her hips and guided her into a new rhythm—forward and backward on his cock so that her clit ground against him. "Want you to come on me."

"Oh, yes," she gasped, her expression almost anguished in her desire. His gaze raked over her pretty face, her swaying breasts, the red hair between her thighs rubbing against his lower belly.

"Come here," he said, pulling her down to his chest. Caden banded an arm around her lower back and one around her neck, pinning her in place on top of him, and then he took over the grind, rubbing himself hard against her clit, his cock still deep inside. "Love being inside you," he whispered. "Love this closeness, with you."

"I'm gonna come. I'm gonna come," she cried.

Caden crashed his lips down on hers and filled her mouth with his tongue. Her whole body bowed on the orgasm, trying to break free from his arms. He held her tight and swallowed the moan that ripped up her throat as her pussy fisted him and fisted him and coated his cock and balls with her pleasure.

Her muscles went limp and she released a long breath. "Holy shit," she rasped. "Your turn. I want to feel you fall apart like that so bad. How do you want it?"

"Lay down on your stomach," he said, need and lust still stalking through his blood. "I'll be quiet, promise." They switched positions, and Caden spread himself out on top of Makenna. He took his cock in hand and entered her from behind. As he penetrated deep, he laid down on top of her, covering her from head to feet, all of him touching all of her.

"Oh, God, I love that," she whispered. "Love your weight on me. Love how filled up I feel."

Her words licked over his skin. "Gonna fuck you so deep, Red," he said against her ear, his hips surging and grinding into her ass.

"So fucking deep." His arms wrapped around her head and shoulders for leverage, and his abs contracted on each thrust, hunching his body quietly around hers. Driving deep, deep, deeper. She arched her back and lifted her ass. "Oh, that's it," he said, balls deep inside her. "That's so fucking it."

"Caden," she breathed. "Jesus."

"Yeah, you're taking me, aren't you? My cock's so deep inside you." But as deep as it was, it wasn't deep enough. Never would be. Because he'd never be able to get enough of her. Not if he lived a hundred lifetimes.

That was how hard he'd fallen for her. The clarity of the thought was startling. For weeks he'd been hiding from the truth of it, not examining it too closely.

He drove the thought away. Not now. Not yet. Not with another man's words pinballing around his brain. He just couldn't... *Just feel. For once, just feel.*

Caden gripped her tighter, drove deeper, clenched his teeth against the grunts that wanted to tear up his throat. He gritted out whispered words into her ear, dirty little nothings that had her core growing tighter around him and his balls aching with the need to release.

"Faster," she whispered. "Faster and I'm gonna come again."

"Fuck, yeah." His hips snapped more quickly, the meeting of their skin making more noise now. But he couldn't hold back, couldn't resist giving her what she needed. And then she was coming once more, a moan spilling from her mouth. He covered her lips with his hand as her body clamped down on his cock. Then his own orgasm nailed him in the back and exploded him apart. He rode her slow and deep as wave after wave of sensation tore through him, not wanting it to end. Ever. "Jesus Christ," he rasped when their bodies finally stilled.

"So sexy to hear you come," she whispered.

"Shit, was I loud?" he asked, his head resting against hers, his heart still racing in his chest.

"No," she said, a smile plain in her voice. "Maybe we should sleep right here. That way if we get horny again, we can just pick up where we left off."

Caden chuckled. "You've got big plans for tonight, huh?"

She grinned over her shoulder. "Where you're concerned? Absolutely."

The words were just light-hearted joking, but he couldn't help but wonder if she meant them more broadly. If her conversation with Cameron was still pinging around inside his head, which it was, then surely it was doing the same to hers. Part of him thought he should tell her he'd overheard it, but part of him wanted her to choose to tell him it had happened. He eased off of her, removed the condom, and wrapped it in a tissue from a box on her nightstand. Then he gave her a hand off the floor and pulled her into his arms.

"Happy Thanksgiving, Caden. I'm so glad I got to spend the day with you. Of everything I have in my life, I hope you know that I'm most grateful for you this year."

He let the words settle like a balm into some of the raw places inside him, and they helped. But in his darkest places, he couldn't stop wondering if what her ex-fiancé had said to her could change that.

～◌～◌～◌～

Caden felt better in the light of the morning. After the incredible lovemaking on Makenna's floor, they'd slept wrapped around one another all night, skin to skin, and both left him feeling claimed, owned, connected. She'd seduced *him* last night. She'd slept with *him* last night. She'd woke up in *his* arms this morning. That's what mattered. Not what Cameron wanted.

Why did the part of his brain that controlled Caden's fears and anxiety have to be so powerful?

No matter.

He could be stronger. For her.

Caden dried off from his shower and tugged on fresh clothes, glad to be back in jeans again. It made him feel more himself. He tugged the soft black Henley over his head, gave himself a onceover in the bathroom mirror, and opened the door to join Makenna downstairs.

Except the sound of his own name in a male's voice had him freezing in place and pushing the door most of the way closed again.

"She said she was serious about Caden, but that she'd think about it." Cameron. "I said my piece. There's nothing else I can do."

"Caden." Ian that time. He said the name with so much disdain that he might as well have said *Fucking Caden*. Their voices came from Ian's room right across the hall from the bathroom. Caden opened his door a little wider so he could hear them. Because if they were going to fucking talk about him, he was going to fucking listen. "If you want her, you need to fight for her. You think *he's* good enough for her? Because I don't. And I can't believe that my brothers do either. Tattoos and piercings all over his face? Did you see how the conversation flat-out halted when she said she was going to get a tattoo? That's all him. Great fucking influence. She deserves better."

Ian's hostility was a sucker punch to the gut, his words slicing deep at those darkest places. Caden's pulse pounded in his ears.

"I agree. It kills me to see her with him. For all those reasons and more. But I laid it all out for her. I didn't hold anything back. If I push her, she might shut me down all the way," Cameron said. "I gotta give her space on this. If it's gonna happen, it has to be her decision this time. She has to come to me."

"I hear you," Ian said, frustration plain in his voice. "You two were just so good together. I know things got messed up, but Makenna was so happy with you. I want that again for her. And for you. You're family. You've been family for twenty years. You deserve this and so does she. I'm glad you had the chance to talk to her, at least."

"Yeah," Cameron said. "Listen, I'm going to cut out before breakfast. I don't want things to be awkward with Makenna, and clearly Caden and I both being here is creating stress for her." There were some shuffling sounds, and then the door across the hallway clicked shut.

"You should be the one staying," Ian said.

Caden nearly held his breath. He pushed the door closed as much as he could without making it click and listened as footsteps and voices crossed to the stairs and disappeared altogether. When they were gone, he secured the door and fell back against it, his head aching, his chest hollow. He scrubbed his hand over the scar running in a crescent over his ear.

Hell if Ian's reaction wasn't exactly what Caden feared from her family. And was Ian right? Did Patrick and Collin feel the same way? Was Mike horrified at the guy his only daughter had brought home? Caden hadn't gotten anything but positive vibes from the other three James men, but maybe his radar was as fucked as his head.

Or maybe Ian was just an asshole. Caden got it, he did. Cameron was his life-long best friend and Ian wanted him to be happy. Fine. Whatever. That was one thing. But to dislike him because he thought Caden unworthy? That was another.

That was his true fear.

Jesus.

Just when he'd managed to get his head screwed on right about Makenna's conversation with Cameron.

Knock, knock.

Caden bowed off the door. "Yeah?" he said, pulling it open.

"Hey, there you are." Makenna's gaze scanned over his face, and her smile dropped into a frown. "Are you okay?"

"Uh, yeah. Yeah. Just finished getting ready." He flicked off the bathroom light.

"Dad's still making breakfast, so I thought maybe we could talk for a minute?" she said.

His gut clenched as dread snaked through him. "Sure. What's up?"

She took his hand, led him back to her room, and closed the door. Caden moved to the center of the room and crossed his arms, braced for the blow. "Are you sure you're okay?" she asked.

"What is it you want to talk about, Makenna?" The words came out more clipped than he'd intended, but he was hanging on by a thread right now. Very thin and fraying in the middle.

"Come sit," she said.

"That's okay." He forced a deep breath and stayed planted right where he was.

She frowned, her gaze studying his face like she was trying to solve a puzzle. "We fell asleep so fast last night that we never had a chance to finish the conversation from the bathroom." Makenna gave him a little smile, clearly trying to coax some reaction from him. "So." She sagged onto the edge of the bed. "The short story is that three years ago, Cameron and I were engaged for about five minutes. It ended when he gave me an ultimatum. I'd landed the job I wanted in DC and he had fellowship offers from hospitals here and in DC. It all could've worked."

Hearing her talk about the life she might've been leading right now—a life with another man—settled a weight onto Caden's shoulders. And the reason why was clear—he was *all in*. All in love with Makenna. Whether he wanted to admit it or not. Whether he wanted to face it or not. Whether he believed that meant certain doom for her or him or both of them, or not.

For fourteen years he'd been alone, purposely keeping others out, purposely living life as a loner, purposely avoiding relationships except with a select few friends. He'd hooked up with women over the years, but he'd purposely distanced himself from the ones who seemed to want more with him. Building a wall around himself had been a survival mechanism after his family had been destroyed, and then it had become a habit, one he'd never even tried to unlearn until Makenna.

"But Cam decided that the fellowship at Penn was more prestigious," she said, staring up at Caden. "And he said if I really loved him, I'd stay in Philly and find another job. Because he wouldn't do a long-distance relationship, so if I wouldn't stay in Philly, the whole relationship was off." She waved a hand. "We had a big fight. But it made me realize he wasn't the right man for me, because the right man would never ask me to give up my dream for his, especially when he had another great and still very prestigious option that would allow both of us to have what we wanted. So I took the job and moved to DC and we just sorta ended."

"Okay," Caden said.

"So that's the backstory." She heaved a deep breath.

He frowned. "The backstory to what?"

"To a conversation I had with Cameron last night that I want you to know about."

Caden swallowed. Hard. As much as he'd wanted her to tell him, now he was scared to hear what might come out of her mouth. "Which was?"

"Cameron asked for a second chance," she said, her fingers fidgeting with the hem of her sweater. "And said he wants to try again and that he still loves me. I wanted you to—"

"Do you still love him?" he forced himself to ask.

She flew off the bed and came right up to him, one of her hands settling on his crossed arms, one cupping his face. "No. Not for a long time. I told him that I'm with you, that I'm serious about you, that it's too late and too much time has passed." Makenna shook her head, her eyes pleading. "You're the only one I...that I have feelings for. I care about you so much, Caden. Please tell me that you know that."

"Are you...are you sure that you don't want to consider what he's offering?" Voicing the question made Caden nauseous, but if he didn't ask her, he'd just wonder about it. Better to get it all out in the open. His anxiety needed to hear her say the words. "He's a high-powered specialist. He'll be able to give you a good life. And he's known your family forever."

Makenna blanched and her whole face frowned. "Oh, my God. I don't want to consider his offer. I don't want him. I want you. I have a great life with you right now. Caden." She forced his arms to part and pressed herself against him, both of her hands cupping his face. "You're the only man I want. You."

For a moment he didn't say anything because he couldn't. Relief made his throat go tight and his chest ache with pressure.

"Do you remember the night we met, before we went to bed? I mentioned how late it had gotten and you thought that was me trying to tell you to go?" Caden nodded. That night had been so amazing with her that he hadn't been able to avoid wondering when the other shoe would drop. He'd thought it had been that moment. "Do you remember what I said?"

"You called bullshit on me," he said, the memory pulling a little of the heaviness off his shoulders.

Makenna smiled. "I totally did. And I said, just so there's no more weirdness or uncertainty, I like you." He nodded, the memory tugging at the corner of his lips. "Well, I'm saying it again right now. Just so there's no more weirdness or uncertainty, I like you. A lot." She nailed him with a stare, her blue eyes blazing.

"Shit. I get caught in my head sometimes, Makenna," he said, throwing out a lifeline.

She caught it. "Oh, Caden, I know you do, but it's okay. I hated to even dump all this on you, but I also didn't want to keep it from you. That didn't feel right."

Knock, knock.

"Yeah?" she called, not letting him break the embrace.

Patrick popped his head in the door. "Dad said breakfast is ready."

"Be right there," Makenna said. Her brother ducked back out. "Are we okay?" she asked.

Caden blew out a breath, some of the tension bleeding out of his body with it. It was just, on top of Ian's comments, he'd been so ready for more bad news. Instead, she'd given him her honesty and understanding, and it made him love her even more. No sense in denying that's what it was anymore.

"Yeah. I'm sorry," he said, feeling a little drained. Life was a lot fucking easier without all these emotions coming at him all the time. Makenna had opened him up, and sometimes it made him feel like an exposed nerve that was too sensitive, too vulnerable, too unprotected.

He was always going to be a lot to take on board, wasn't he?

"You don't have anything to be sorry for," she said. "I'm sorry you even have to deal with any of this."

"No, I'm glad you told me," he said. And he was.

Sometimes his brain got stuck on a loop of negativity, spiraling him down and down and down, and having her words saying the things she'd said was the best cure for when that happened. He needed her words, just like he'd needed them that night they'd been trapped in the elevator. Then they'd kept him from succumbing to his claustrophobia. Now they kept him from handing a microphone to his darkest fears so they could convince him those fears were real. Both times, she'd pulled him back from the brink.

"And for the record, I like you, too. A lot." His feelings ran deeper than that, obviously, but he was too bare, too raw, to contemplate confronting his fears by saying anything more just then.

Her smile was radiant. "Best thing I've heard all day." She rested her hands on his chest. "Look, if you want to go back to Virginia, we could leave today. I know Cameron being here made this trip more stressful than it should've been."

Caden immediately shook his head. "No. No way. I'm enjoying your family." Well, most of them. "And I know you love being here. I don't want to go home early." No way would he do that to her. He knew how important her family was to her.

"I would go, for you." Earnest blue eyes stared up at him.

He knew she would, and it was part of why he loved her. He shook his head. "And I'm staying for you."

CHAPTER SEVEN

Despite the rocky start to the morning, Makenna had a great day with Caden and her family. Breakfast, a late lunch full of yummy leftovers, and an afternoon of board games that had everyone laughing and teasing. With Cameron gone, the whole atmosphere changed from tense to easy, at least that was the way it felt to her. She was itching to confront Ian about inviting him, but she didn't want to create new tension. It could wait until after the holiday.

It was late as their group walked out of the movie theater after seeing the last showing of a new action flick, their bellies full of Chinese food and popcorn—everyone had been ready for a change of menu after several meals in a row of turkey and stuffing. The sidewalks were crunchy with rock salt and patches of ice that hadn't been shoveled away.

Four inches of snow had fallen yesterday, which wasn't bad for Pennsylvania. But then freezing rain had fallen over night after the streets had been plowed, so driving had been more hazardous today then it'd been yesterday, but luckily her dad and Caden hadn't minded bringing them out to the movies.

"Be safe heading home, kids," her dad called as he, Ian, Collin, and Shima passed Caden's Jeep and headed over to Dad's Ford Explorer.

"Will do," Caden said, unlocking the doors. Makenna hopped in the back seat so Patrick could have the front.

Yawning, Makenna secured her seatbelt and sagged back against the seat as Caden pulled out of the lot. He followed her dad's car through the commercial area around the mall to where the surroundings became surburban and then almost rural-looking on the way to their house.

As the lights receded, Makenna's eyelids grew heavy. And against the backdrop of Caden and Patrick talking, she finally stopped fighting it and let herself drift off.

A sudden jerk startled Makenna awake. Screeching tires. The Jeep fishtailed hard in one direction and then the other.

"Fuck," Patrick bit out.

The Jeep came to a hard stop, jolting Makenna against her seatbelt and knocking the breath out of her.

Both men seat turned to her. "Are you okay?" they asked.

"Yeah. What happened?" Her eyes focused on the scene out the front window. Two cars sat just off the road at an intersection. One was an Explorer. "Oh, my God. Dad." She ripped at the seat belt buckle.

"Makenna, call 9-1-1. Patrick and I will check it out," Caden said. He flew out of the driver's seat, ran to the trunk and grabbed something, and then ran toward the accident. Patrick was already opening her father's car door.

She pressed the phone to her ear as she jumped out of the Jeep. Caden had managed to stop in plenty of time, his Jeep just off the road. He'd placed an orange cone at the back corner of his vehicle.

"Nine-one-one, what is your emergency?" the dispatcher answered.

"I'm calling to report an accident," Makenna said, jogging toward the scene, heart racing. She recounted what'd happened and let the dispatcher know that an off-duty police officer and paramedic were on scene.

"Can you put me on with either of them when they've assessed for injuries?" the dispatcher asked.

"Yes. Let me get them," Makenna said. She didn't know how either Patrick or Caden did this kind of thing every day, because just the act of calling 911 had adrenaline flowing through her system until she was shivering. It was more than just the cold, she knew that much for sure. Dread flowing through her, she approached the driver's side of her father's truck and could see that the front end was crumpled.

Patrick leaned into her father's door while Caden stood in the rear driver's side doorway, a big medic kit opened next to him. She peered in to see Collin, bleeding from the forehead and grimacing. Oh God.

"The dispatcher would like to talk to one of you," she said.

Patrick held out his hand, and she passed him the phone. He rose and stepped away from the vehicle.

Makenna leaned in and gently touched her father's arm. The air bags had deployed inside the car. "Daddy, are you okay?"

"Yeah, yeah, peanut. The seatbelt just took the wind out of me. I'll be fine," he said, his voice like gravel.

"Hang tight, Collin. I don't want you to move until we can get your neck immobilized, okay?" Caden asked, snapping off one pair of gloves and putting on another. "Let me check your dad. I'll be right back."

Makenna stepped away to let Caden pass and Ian came around from the passenger side. "Are you okay?" she asked him.

"Yeah. Shima and I are fine. Collin didn't have his seat belt on, though," Ian said, the words not critical, just worried.

As she watched, Caden listened to her father's heartbeat and took his pulse, and then he unbuttoned her father's shirt and examined his chest in the dim overhead light.

"How are they?" Patrick asked Caden, phone still pressed to his ear.

"Collin has a mild head injury, a scalp lac, and a probable rib fracture," Caden said in a calm, confident voice. Makenna's chest squeezed with worry as Patrick relayed the information to the dispatcher. Caden continued, "Mike has an elevated heart rate and chest pain reproducible on palpitation and movement, which means a possible sternum fracture. At least, that's what I can tell without more diagnostics."

God, both of them needed to go to the hospital. Makenna couldn't believe this was happening. Her brother repeated Caden's diagnosis.

"EMS is within range," Patrick said. "I hear the sirens."

Makenna had just cued in to them, too.

"All right, Mike. Cavalry's almost here. They'll get some pain meds in you and you'll be good as new. Just try to sit still," Caden said.

"Thanks, son. I'm okay," her dad said, the strain in his voice belying the words.

Caden snapped off his gloves and moved to the back seat again. As worried as she was about her father and brother, she was also fascinated to see Caden in action—confident, totally in control, rushing in to help without having to be asked. Exactly what he was trained to do.

A few minutes later, two police cars, two ambulances, and a firetruck rumbled into the scene, their red and blue lights circling over everything. As the crews got out of their vehicles, Patrick met up with the police and Caden joined the paramedics as they unloaded stretchers and backboards from the rear of their rig. He was deep in conversation with them, clearly recounting what he'd learned about the men's conditions.

Makenna leaned into the driver's seat. "The ambulance is here. Just hang on," she said.

Her father gave her a tight smile. "Don't you worry."

When the paramedics approached the car, Shima cleared out of the back seat, and one of the paramedics went around and took her place, the other leaning in through Collin's doorway like Caden had done.

Makenna and Ian stepped back too, making space for the crews to do their job. Caden fell in beside her, his gaze running over her face. "Are you sure you're okay?" he asked, taking her cheek in his hand. "I know you were asleep when it happened. I tried to stop as gently as I could."

"I'm fine. Really. What happened?"

Caden frowned. "The damn ice. The second driver tried to pull out of the cross street without sufficient lead time and his back tires caught ice, which stalled him half-way out. So your dad had to swerve to avoid him, but he hit a patch of ice, too, and caught the vehicle's back quarter panel before going off the road."

"It was lucky Dad responded so quickly," Ian said. "I thought for sure we were going to broad-side him."

Nodding, Caden said, "It could've been a lot worse, that's for sure."

"It's bad enough," Makenna said, her throat going tight.

"Come here," Caden said, pulling her into his chest. "They're going to be all right. You'll see."

"Thanks to you," she said, peering up at him. "This would've been so much scarier if you weren't here."

He shook off the compliment and rubbed her back.

Soon, the two paramedic crews had Dad and Collin loaded onto stretchers. They told Caden where they were going and said the family would have to follow by separate vehicle. As the crews loaded the stretchers into their rigs, Patrick waved Ian and Shima over to the police, who seemed to be asking them questions.

Patrick joined her and Caden. "You four go ahead to the hospital. I'll finish up here and one of these guys will give me a lift home to get my car when we're done."

"Okay," Caden said. The two men shook.

"Thanks for everything, Caden. It means a lot," Patrick said. "Keep me posted."

"We will. Wish I could've done more," he said.

When Ian, Shima, and Caden had given statements, they loaded up into Caden's Jeep and made the quiet drive to the hospital. Shima sat next to Makenna, concern radiating off of her, and it touched her to know how deeply concerned Shima was for her brother. She really cared.

But getting to the hospital didn't give them any answers, because while Dad and Collin were being evaluated, all the rest of them could do was wait. Within an hour, Patrick had come, but they still hadn't heard from anyone in the emergency department beyond filling out some forms on both the James men's behalves.

Caden was a godsend through it all. Grabbing coffee for all of them. Staying close to Makenna's side. Holding her hand. Explaining to everyone what was likely happening to Dad and Collin respectively so they'd all understand why it was taking so long—the scans they both required were probably part of the hold-up.

This would've been so much harder if Caden hadn't been there. More than that, it felt like he *belonged* there. As part of the James clan. At her side.

"Mike and Collin James family," called a woman's voice.

They all stood at once, her and Patrick going fastest to join the woman near the doors to the ER.

"I can only allow one person back for each patient," she said.

Makenna turned to Ian. "Do you mind if I go with Patrick?"

"No," Ian said. "Just text me when you know more."

Giving Caden a quick hug and a kiss, Makenna agreed. She gave Shima a nod, too. "Will let you all know as soon as we can." And then she was rushing to her father and youngest brother's sides, heart in her throat to know that they were going to be okay. She couldn't lose any of these men that she loved. Not her father, not her brothers, and not Caden.

Because the pain of it would absolutely shatter her.

CHAPTER EIGHT

It was morning before they got home. Turned out Makenna's dad didn't have a sternum fracture; he was just badly bruised—which was good news. Collin did have a broken rib, but his head scans had been clear and the scalp lac didn't include any injury to the bone beneath. When they got back to the James house, everyone helped get Mike and Collin settled before falling into bed.

"You were my hero last night, you know that?" Makenna said, half asleep next to Caden in her small bed. Even exhausted she was so damn beautiful, with the morning light bringing out all the shades of red in her hair.

Caden shook his head. He'd never be comfortable with that word. Hero. Because he was always questioning if he'd done enough, been good enough. Heroes were brave and fearless, neither of which described his anxiety-ridden ass. He knew himself well enough to know that was true. "I was…just doing my job. It's what I do."

"That doesn't make it any less heroic," she said, rolling closer so that her chin rested on his bare chest. Makenna traced her finger over his rose tattoo. "People live because you get up and go to work, Caden. That's…that's amazing."

There was truth in what she said, but it still made him uncomfortable to think about it that way. He always thought of it more as a debt owed, as paying back the universe for what someone had done for him. And not just anyone, but David Talbot. That was the name of the paramedic who had first arrived on the scene of his family's accident fourteen years before. That was the name of the man who'd saved Caden's life and pulled him back from the brink of madness.

Their car had flipped into an irrigation ditch that ran along the side of a country road, making it so that passing cars couldn't see it in the darkness. For hours, Caden had been pinned upside down in the back seat, his head wedged between the front center console and passenger seat, his shoulder dislocated, something stabbing him in the side.

He'd called out his family's names for a long time, but no one ever answered. He'd screamed for help every time the lights of a passing car flickered through the gloom, but no one ever came.

Caden had passed in and out of consciousness for hours until he could no longer distinguish reality from nightmare. By the time a long-haul trucker finally stopped in the early light of morning, Caden hadn't responded to the man's calls to see if everyone was all right because he hadn't believed the voice was real.

His mind hadn't stopped playing tricks on him ever since.

"I'm just glad I could help," he finally said, leaning up to kiss Makenna on the forehead. He ran his fingers through her soft hair. He never had tired of playing with it, and didn't think he ever would. "Let's get some sleep."

Makenna kissed his chest and pressed herself tight along the side of his body, her head on his shoulder. They fell asleep quickly, but the combination of the accident and the anxiety caused by the overheard conversations had twisted his subconscious into knots that played out in some of the worst nightmares he'd had in years.

They all started out the same—with his father losing control of the car and it flipping in a series of crushing, body-bruising jolts until it finally landed upside down, the impact throwing Caden's body so hard that he became pinned in place, unable to move.

It was the endings that were different.

In one, no one ever came to rescue Caden from the accident, and he was still there now—a living hell he could never escape, blood still dripping down over his face from the wound on his head.

In another, his brother Sean's eyelids flipped open in his lifeless face, his eyes sightless in death but so accusing as they stared at Caden. Sean moaned, "It shoulda been me. I shoulda been the one to live," before disappearing into thin air.

In the one that just had him gasping awake, it was Ian who first showed up on the scene, and when he looked in and saw Caden hanging there, he just said, "She deserves better than you," and walked away as Caden screamed and screamed.

Jesus.

Caden looked to his side to find that Makenna had turned over at some point. She must've been exhausted for his bullshit not to have disturbed her, because he knew his nightmares often woke her up. Just another thing he hated about himself, for her sake.

He blew out a long breath. Caden was so fucking exhausted. And it was an exhaustion that had absolutely nothing to do with last night's lack of sleep. It was an exhaustion he carried in his very soul, one that weighed down his spirit with grief and survivor's guilt and self-doubt, and he didn't know how he'd ever fix that. Or what it should mean if he couldn't.

Finally, Makenna stirred beside him. "Hey," she said, giving him a sleepy smile.

God, she was so very pretty. It struck him dumb every time. "Hey."

"Did you sleep?" she asked.

"Yeah," he said. Some, anyway. If she hadn't heard his nightmares, he didn't need to burden her with them.

"I must not have slept enough," she said, making a face. "I'm kinda nauseous."

"It's three o'clock in the afternoon," Caden said. "We've missed two meals. Maybe food will help."

They threw on clothes and found Mike, Patrick, and Ian congregated around the island in the kitchen.

"Daddy," Makenna said, rushing up to him. "How are you feeling?"

He huffed out a little laugh. "A little beat-up, but I'll be okay, peanut."

"I wish I could stay longer," she said, leaning her head against her father. With a grimace, Mike put his arm around her and softly hugged her in. The gesture was so casual in its intimacy and tenderness that it stole Caden's breath. Not because there was anything particularly unique about a father hugging his child, but because after the accident, Caden's father never once hugged him again.

The accident had left his old man with his own demons, leaving no room for the father-son relationship they'd once had. And it had made a much younger version of himself believe that his own father wished Caden hadn't survived either. He'd felt like such a burden to the man, for years. It was part of why he'd started donning the armor of his ink.

"Don't you worry about it," Mike said. "Collin and I are going to be fine."

"Do you want to stay and take the train home when you're ready?" Caden asked. He felt bad that his having to work tomorrow cut the weekend short, but the price of getting the holiday off was a series of back-to-back twenty-four/seven shifts for the next few days.

Makenna blew out a breath and braced her hand on the counter. "I don't know. I have to work on Monday anyway."

"Are you okay?" Patrick asked. "You're kinda green."

"No sleep and no food," she said.

"What do you want?" Caden asked. "I'll make you something."

"We were just talking about food, too," Mike said. "We still have plenty of leftovers."

"Why don't you two go sit down?" Caden said to Mike and Makenna. "We can take charge of dinner." He looked at Patrick.

"Absolutely," Patrick said.

Makenna pressed up onto tiptoes to give Caden a quick kiss as she passed him. "Thank you." It was the first time they'd done something more than hold hands or sit close together in front of everyone, and Caden braced for a reaction. But there was none. Not even from Ian, who'd been very quiet around him since the accident.

The three of them heated up the food and set it out on the table. And even though Ian's derisive words were still pinging around the back of Caden's brain, he liked this family. Despite Ian's snubs. Mike was loving and friendly and generous. Patrick was a good guy and a straight shooter, and they worked together as well in the kitchen as they had on the scene the night before. Collin was talkative and funny, easy going and accepting. And Makenna…Makenna was everything good and light and loving.

Soon they were all gathered around to eat, including Collin and Shima, who came down when the smells of turkey and stuffing started wafting through the house. Collin was moving a little stiffly and looking a little bleary-eyed but otherwise he'd be fine. And Caden was glad. He'd hate to see anything happen to the family Makenna loved so much. Because she deserved everything.

The meal was subdued compared to the conversation of the day before, but it was real. Real life. And for the first time, Caden actually let himself imagine being a part of it.

The past couple of days had kicked Makenna's butt. First, the unexpected conversation with Cameron. Then, the accident. Then, the stomach virus she'd picked up that had left her queasy and exhausted. And finally, she'd barely seen Caden in the four days since they'd gotten home because he'd had back-to-back shifts that had allowed him to get the holiday off in the first place.

All of which made her very glad that they'd have tonight together. He'd made the arrangements for her to get her first tattoo, and Makenna was thrilled. And a little nervous. Okay, a lot nervous. But Caden would be right there with her.

The work day finally over, Makenna took the elevator to the first floor—her favorite elevator, the one that made her smile every time she took it because she'd met Caden in it—and made her way to the Metro. Outside, it was already dark, and the cold air bit at her skin. But she was all pure frenetic energy looking forward to tonight.

Back at her apartment, she was thrilled to find Caden home. Wearing jeans and an ACFD T-shirt, he was in the kitchen unpacking containers from plastic bags. "Hey," she said. "What smells so good?"

"Hey, Red," he said in a quiet voice. He turned toward her. For a split second, something in his gaze looked wrong, almost disheartened, but then he gave a little smile and his whole face changed. "I stopped at the noodle place."

"You okay?" she asked, wrapping her arms around his neck.

"Yeah," he said, hugging her back. "Last night's shift was non-stop and I couldn't seem to stay asleep today."

"Ugh, I'm sorry," she said. "Well, thank you for getting food. I love the noodle place." *And I love you.*

She thought it so often these days that the words lived on the tip of her tongue. After the conversation about Cameron, Makenna had been so tempted to just tell Caden how she felt, but there'd been moments over the weekend where he'd seemed stressed, and she could tell he was at his limit. They'd get there. She knew they would. The way he looked at her, the way he took care of her, the way he made love to her—it all said he felt the same way she did, even if he hadn't given her the words.

"I know," he said with a wink. "That's why I stopped there." His lips found hers, warm and exploring. She reveled in the little bites of his piercings against her skin as he kissed her again and again.

"Mmm, good appetizer," she said around the edge of the kiss.

He grinned. "Food then tattoo. Then we can come back to appetizers after."

"Fine," she said, feigning being put out. "I guess I can live with that plan."

"You excited?" he asked, returning to the counter.

Makenna couldn't hold back her smile. "Really excited. Heath sent me the final version of the design today," she said. "Wanna see it?"

"Of course," he said, grabbing silverware from a drawer. Heath was the tattoo artist who'd done most of Caden's work over the years. "He's great, isn't he?"

She dropped her bags on the edge of the counter and fished out the sketch. She found the sheet and made sure it was the right one before she handed it to Caden—because she had two versions of it in her bag. One for Caden to see, and one that Heath was actually going to use to make the stencil. She'd cooked up a little surprise that he couldn't know about until the ink was done, and she was nearly bursting at the seams.

Caden studied the design for a long moment. "This is fantastic, Makenna. How big are you thinking?"

"That's the size," she said, imagining what it was going to look like in the center of her upper back. The circle surrounding the Celtic knot tree was about five inches round. At first, she'd thought she wanted it to be smaller, but Heath had talked her into a somewhat bigger piece so that the holes in the center of all the knot work would remain distinct as the tattoo aged.

"It's gonna be fucking beautiful. But then, it'll be on you, so of course it will." He leaned down and gave her a nuzzling kiss on the cheek. "Do you want to get changed and I'll set everything out?"

"Yeah," she said. "Sounds great." The kitchen, dining area, and living room were one big room, with her bedroom door toward the far end. She paused there and looked back. Caden moved around her little kitchen, comfortably and familiarly, and he just looked so freaking good there. In her space. Well, *their* space now.

He still had his townhouse in Fairlington, but he rarely slept there anymore. And it was so bare bones in furnishings that he preferred they not sleep there because he feared she'd be uncomfortable. A part of her wasn't sure why he even kept it at this point.

"What?" he asked, giving her a skeptical look.

She grinned and leaned against the door jamb. "I rode our elevator today."

He shook his head. "Anything interesting happen?"

"Oh, I got trapped with a smoking hot stranger and made out with him in the dark. The usual," she said.

He smirked. "That never happens."

Makenna threw her head back and laughed. Still smiling, she changed into jeans and a pink camisole with a low back, and then she threw a warm, chunky caramel-colored cardigan over that.

She found Caden sitting at the set table, containers of food overflowing with several types of noodles. It smelled amazing—savory and spicy and like she could eat everything she saw.

For a moment, the look on his face made her think he was upset about something, but then he saw her and his expression transformed into a sexy smirk. "Smoking hot, huh?"

Laughing, she took the seat next to him. "You fishing for compliments, Grayson? I already said you were freaking gorgeous."

"Yeah, but that's not the same as smoking hot." He arched a brow, and damn if his playfully smug, expectant expression wasn't hot as hell with his brow piercing and the widow's peak of his dark hair.

She picked up her fork. "Okay, then how about this? You are so freaking gorgeous and so smoking hot that you make my heart race and my mouth water and my panties melt. Every time I see you. How's that for a compliment?"

Caden's smile was slow coming but so damn sexy. "I like tattoo night."

She laughed and shook her head. "So do I."

CHAPTER NINE

Heroic Ink was located on the edge of Old Town Alexandria, the oldest part of the town that had started as a port back in colonial times. Located on a quaint street full of boutiques and restaurants, the tattoo studio had a well-known reputation for its expertise in military tattoos of all kinds, which explained all the military memorabilia and photographs of service men and woman tacked in a giant collage to the front of the registration desk.

When they walked in the front door, the blue-haired woman at the desk recognized Caden right away. "Well, hey you," she said. "It's been way too long."

"I know, I know," Caden said, his hand at the small of Makenna's back. "Rachel, this is Makenna James. She's here for Heath."

"Hi Makenna," Rachel said, holding out a heavily tattooed hand. "So nice to meet you."

Makenna smiled and shook Rachel's hand. The woman was stunning and so cool. With short two-toned blue hair, a nose piercing, and ink everywhere, you could look at her for an hour and not take everything in. And she had such an inviting smile. "Hi Rachel. I'm excited to be here."

"This is your first one?" she asked, placing a form on a clipboard in front of her.

"Yes." She grinned at Caden, who was totally watching her as she took everything in.

"Well, let's get this party started," Rachel said.

Before long, Makenna was seated backward on a chair, her hair twisted up in a knot on the top of her head, and Heath was applying the stencil to the center of her upper back, just below her neck.

Heath was kind of the quiet type, which probably explained why he and Caden got along. But he could also be funny and wickedly sarcastic, and he was cute besides. He had short brown hair and a full beard and moustache, and lots of ink peaked out beneath his band T-shirt and holey jeans.

Heath handed her a mirror. "Want to check out the placement?"

Makenna walked to the full-length mirror near her chair and looked over her shoulder. Butterflies raced through her belly. The design was beautiful and she loved it, but a part of her couldn't believe she was having this done. She never would've been brave enough to do this without Caden.

She didn't mind when he walked up to look, because Heath was leaving her little surprise off until he was almost ready to do it.

"What do you think?" she asked Caden as she studied the design in the mirror. Beneath the tree, the roots were made up of the initials M, E, P, I, M, C—for the six members of the James family, including her mother, Erin. "I think it looks perfect."

"So do I," he said, his gaze fixed on her skin. "You ready?"

"So ready," she said.

The kiss he gave her was deep and wet. He whispered in her ear, "I'm already getting turned on thinking about you getting inked."

Well now *she* was turned on. "Appetizers after, remember?"

He nodded, his crooked smile bringing one of his dimples out to play.

Heath gave her a few instructions and then his tattoo machine came to life on a low buzz. "Let me know if you need a break. This one's going to take a little while, so it's completely fine." From the corner of her eye, she caught him dipping the tip into a little cup of black ink, and then leaned in, his gloved hand falling on her back.

Makenna bit her lip at the first contact of the needles. It kinda hurt, like something almost sharp scratching you, but it was tolerable. "Not too bad," she said to Caden, who was sitting in a chair right in front of her.

"There will be more sensitive places, but nothing you can't handle," he said, his dark eyes full of a sexy look that was part pride, part satisfaction, and part lust. Appetizers were going to be *good*.

"How you doing, Makenna?" Heath asked.

"Good," she said, staring at Caden. "No problem."

"So Caden said you two met in an elevator," Heath said, amusement plain in his voice.

"We really did. We were trapped in it for over four hours," Makenna said, smiling. It was a little weird to talk to someone she couldn't look at, but she couldn't move while he was working. "In my office building. I rode it just today."

"That's quite a way to meet someone," Heath said with a chuckle. "How come nothing like that ever happens to me?"

"Maybe you don't ride enough elevators," Makenna said.

The tattoo machine pulled away from her skin. Heath laughed. "I guess I don't," he finally said, leaning back in.

The needles hit a sensitive spot along her spine that had Makenna grimacing. Originally, she'd been thinking of putting the piece on her shoulder, but when she'd decided on the bigger size, she thought it would look better in the center. Heath had warned her that the central placement meant inking over bone, which could hurt more, and it sure did.

Caden braced his elbows on his knees so he could lean closer. "Want to play twenty questions?" he asked.

She smiled, knowing he was trying to distract her and appreciating the heck out of the gesture. "Are there still questions left we haven't asked each other?"

"Probably," he said. "For example, I don't think I've ever asked you your favorite sex position."

"No laughing," Heath said, as Makenna tried to hold back her humor. Heat filled her cheeks. "Also, TMI. However, I like TMI, so feel free to answer, Makenna."

Since the needle was away from her skin, she did laugh that time. "Okay, so maybe there are questions we haven't asked." She winked at Caden as Heath got back to work. "And, to answer the question, the second part of the night on my floor."

Caden's gaze went molten. He flicked at the spider bite piercings with his tongue. And that had parts of *her* going molten, because she knew how freaking talented that tongue was.

"Yours?" she asked, arching an eyebrow.

"The same night, but the first position," he said, flicking at his piercing again. So, his favorite was her on top of him. That had been hot too. The position gave her a fantastic view of so much of his ink and all of his piercings, not to mention his darkly handsome face as she took him into her body again and again. She could still hear his voice saying, *Ride me, Makenna. Use me.* And just the memory made her need to squirm in her seat.

"What's your favorite holiday and why?" she asked.

"Thanksgiving," he said immediately. "Because this Thanksgiving was the best of any holiday I've had in years. Almost the best I can remember."

Aw. That answer hit her right in the chest and made those words want to jump off her tongue again. "Mine has always been

Thanksgiving, too. Although Christmas is a close second. Those are the holidays that always bring family together again."

Caden nodded. "What is one thing you'd change about your life if you could?"

She studied him for a moment, wondering if this was just a playful question in the game or if he was still wondering about her feelings for Cameron. But the answer was an easy one. "I wouldn't change anything about my life."

Eyebrow arched, he gave her a skeptical look. "There has to be something."

Makenna thought about it for a long moment, then took a few seconds to breathe through another sensitive patch of skin. "Um, then, I would've wanted my mother to have lived longer so I could've known her. But then, honestly, if she had lived I wonder if my relationship with my father would've been as close. I would hate to lose that. Do I get to ask that one back?" She didn't want to put him on the spot in front of Heath, but he'd asked the question and had to know she'd want to ask it of him, too. That was how they'd played this game in the elevator that night, the game that had helped bring them so close together.

He gave a tight nod and waved a hand at himself. "I'd get rid of the anxiety and the claustrophobia and all that bullshit."

"I get that," she said, hating that he wanted to change anything about himself when she loved him *so much* just as he was. She didn't want perfect, she just wanted him. In all his gorgeous, funny, considerate, and sometimes angsty glory. "But you do realize, if you hadn't been claustrophobic the day we met, you might not have asked me to talk to you in that elevator. You might not have needed my help, and then we might not have gotten to know each other."

He tilted his head, his eyes narrowing in a way that brought out the harshness in that utterly masculine face. Finally, he gave her another nod. "Fair enough. Your turn."

Wanting to lighten the mood, she thought of something funny to ask. "What's your favorite line from *The Princess Bride*?" She was already smiling as some of her favorites came to mind. Funny movies of all kinds were their thing.

Caden grinned. "When Vizzini says, 'Inconceivable!' And Montoya says, 'You keep saying that word. I do not think it means what you think it means.' Oh, or maybe when Vizzini says, 'Stop rhyming and I mean it,' and Fezzik replies—"

"Anybody want a peanut?" all three of them said in unison. The needle pulled away from her skin and they all laughed.

"There are too many good ones in that movie," Heath said.

"It's true," Makenna said, her cheeks hurting from smiling. "I like the priest who pronounces 'marriage' as 'mawage,' and of course the classic, 'My name is Inigo Montoya. You killed my father—"

"Prepare to die," they all said again to more laughter.

The questions went on for a long while. They talked about silly stuff like favorite ice cream flavor, what they'd eat for their last meal, and what other countries they'd want to visit, since neither of them had ever been outside the States. They asked about more serious stuff like what job they'd want if they couldn't do their current one and what the top items on their bucket lists were. As always, the conversation was fun and engaging, animated and moving. They'd always given great talk.

"I'm about two-thirds done," Heath said. "Let's take a little break."

"Okay," Makenna said, standing up to stretch. She was tempted to look in the mirror, but she really wanted to wait to see the finished tattoo.

Caden stepped to her side as if to look.

She whirled away. "You get to see when I get to see—when it's done," she said, not knowing if Heath had added the part Caden didn't know about.

"So it's like that, is it?" he asked with a smirk.

"It's exactly like that." She gave him some smirk right back.

"You're doing great, you know," he said. "It's a big tattoo for your first time."

She checked to make sure Heath wasn't right behind her, and then said. "I like it big. You should know this."

The smile he gave her said he wanted to devour her. "Is it time for appetizers yet?"

"Ready to wrap this up?" Heath said, sitting down on his rolling stool again.

"Definitely," Makenna said, taking her seat. "And for the record, Caden, it's almost time."

Caden had really enjoyed sharing this experience with Makenna, and he was still kinda blown away by the fact that she wanted to do it in the first place. He knew that she really liked his tattoos, but she'd told him that she'd always been afraid they would hurt. And here she'd barely reacted the whole time.

He wasn't surprised, though. Makenna was soft and sweet, but she could also be tough when she needed to be—like when she was calling him on his bullshit, or like how she was so well adjusted about the death of her mother.

"There," Heath said after a while. "All done."

The smile Makenna wore absolutely owned Caden. It really did.

"Can I see it now?" she asked. Heath handed her the mirror, and she walked kinda backward toward the full-length. "I get to see it first," she said, grinning at him and sticking out her tongue. For a long moment, she studied herself, moving the hand-held mirror this way and that, and then her eyes went glassy. "I really love it," she said. "Heath, you are so talented. It's amazing." Her joy was palpable, and it lit Caden up inside.

"Caden, I like this woman a lot. You're welcome to bring her around absolutely any time," he said with a wink.

Makenna laughed. "I mean it, it's great. So much better than I even imagined."

"Well, you're welcome," Heath said.

"Do I get to see it now?" Caden asked, curiosity getting the best of him.

"You do," she said, her expression suddenly shy. She turned around, and Caden came closer.

The black ink was stunning against her fair skin. And she was right, Heath's work was meticulous as always, crisp and clean and executed perfectly. The Celtic knots were beautiful, and the way the tree blended with them was interesting and unique. Across the bottom, six initials in an old-looking font formed a curve among the tree's roots—M, E, P, I, M, C. Caden looked closer. The second M had a smaller letter hanging off of it on a little flourish. C.

"Say something," she said.

He met her gaze in the mirror. "It's incredible," he said. "And it looks fantastic on you, just like I knew it would. What's the little letter C?" That hadn't been on the design she'd shown him earlier.

Meeting his gaze in the mirror, her expression went so, so soft, and she gave a shy little shrug. "The C…is for you."

The words hung there for a moment, and it was like the room sucked in on him. "For me?" he heard himself say as if from a distance. Blood rushed through his ears.

She nodded.

"But…but this…this is your family tree," he said, the room going a little Tilt-a-Whirl around him.

In an instant, she was right in front of him, hands on his chest and bright blue eyes staring up at him. "To me, it feels like you *are* part of my family, Caden. And I wanted you there."

"I…I…don't know…." He shook his head, entirely overwhelmed and overcome. "I mean, that's amazing of you to do. I just can't believe you did it," he said, not exactly sure what he was saying.

And then something else occurred to him. She'd put his initial on her body. It wasn't exactly the same as his name, but close enough. And he'd always heard that tattooing a lover's name jinxed the relationship. It was bad luck. And for him, was there any other kind?

It was a stupid superstition, of course. But it was like him resisting telling her "I love you" because he didn't want to tempt the fates, or the gods of mayhem, or whoever was responsible for bad things happening to good people. His brain was already imagining the ways that little curve of a C could be easily changed into something else—a heart, a clover, another knot.

And Jesus, here he was thinking about not wanting to tell her that he loved her when she'd permanently claimed him on her very skin.

"No one's ever done something like that for me, Makenna," he finally managed, his brain still only vaguely connected to his mouth. "It's…it's amazing."

Her smile was pure joy. "I hope you don't mind. Once I thought of it, it just felt so right. So I went with it. You'll always be a part of me."

"Let's get you bandaged up," Heath said, waving her over to the chair again.

Caden watched him work on Makenna and listened to him give her aftercare instructions, but he did it all as if he was watching it from across the room, from somewhere outside his body. His heart raced and his chest went tight.

Clearly, the tattoo of his initial plucked at his anxiety, but what he said was true—no one had ever done something this special for him. Ever. It was just that, *offuckingcourse*, that made him scared.

Terrified, actually.

After everything he'd lost, how could he have something so, so good for keeps?

CHAPTER TEN

Caden was ravenous for Makenna the minute they walked through her apartment door. He was on her in an instant. Pressing her back against the kitchen counter. Dropping her purse to the floor. Tugging off her coat.

He was using her. He knew he was. Using her to help shut down all the bullshit in his head. Because when he was with her, when he was *in* her, it all went away. It always fucking went away.

But she seemed to be right there with him. Shoving off his jacket, burrowing her hands under his shirt, jerking it up. They worked it off together.

Their kisses were urgent, deep, rough. He devoured her—her skin, her tongue, her moans. He couldn't get enough of her.

"Still…too…many…clothes," Makenna rasped around the edge of a kiss, her hands pulling at the button to his jeans.

"God, I need you," he said, his mind an overwhelming blur, his chest still too tight from before.

"I'm right here," she whispered. "Right here."

But for how long?

The thought came out of nowhere and struck him stupid. He froze, then blinked. As if someone had just unexpectedly punched him in the face.

"Caden?" Breathing heavily, lips swollen, Makenna peered up at him in the dim glow thrown off by a light mounted on the bottom of one of the cabinets.

He hoped the dimness hid the parts of him he didn't want her to see. Like the darkness had in the elevator.

"Need you," he said again, diving back into the kiss. He pulled her with him as he walked them haltingly toward her bedroom. They were a tangle of hands and kisses and shedding clothes. By the time they'd reached the bed, Caden was hard and aching and desperate to bury himself inside her.

"Condom. Hurry," she said.

He couldn't have agreed more. He had it on in a flash and then he turned her to face the bed. "Kneel," he rasped.

Makenna crawled onto the bed, her back arching so fucking beautifully, her ass right there and waiting. Her tattoo flashing at him from under the protective plastic wrap in the ambient light coming in through the window.

He couldn't wait.

He couldn't.

Taking his cock in hand, he found her opening and pushed home. She took all of him. Just like she always did.

Buried deep, her body accepting every bit of him, her moans proclaiming her pleasure, all the noise between his ears ceased. Just fucking went quiet.

And it was such a relief that all he could do was give in to the goddamned incredible perfection of it.

His hips started moving, slower at first, but quickly faster, chasing, needing. He grabbed hold of her hip with one hand and her shoulder with the other, his focus centered on her tattoo—on his C. On the way she'd claimed him when he couldn't even—

No.

He slammed his eyes shut and focused on the slick friction of her body accepting his, on the softness of her skin against his. The sounds of harsh breathing and colliding bodies and the stream of moans spilling from her lips filled the room, and he focused on those, too.

It did the job. Too well. Because out of nowhere his orgasm was an unstoppable force. "Fuck, I'm coming," he gritted out. His cock jerked with each spasm, his hips moving in punctuated thrusts as it played out. He was almost numb from the intensity of it. "Shit, I'm sorry," he said, easing out of her. It was the first time in all the times they'd been together that he hadn't taken care of Makenna first.

Because you weren't really with *her just then, were you?*

She turned onto her side, her smile apparent in the dimness. "Why would you apologize? That was freaking hot."

He disposed of the condom, then returned to her on the bed. "Let me make it up to you, Red," he said, slipping in behind her, his hand sliding over her hip.

"Caden, maybe you can't see the blissed-out expression on my face in the darkness, but trust me, I'm not complaining right now." Humor was plain in her voice, which meant she hadn't clued in to how out of it he was.

"I want you to come," he whispered in her ear, making sure he didn't press against her tattoo. It would be tender for a few days. He pulled her thigh over his, opening her core to his touch. "I always want you to come." She was wet and hot, and her hips pressed into his fingers as they swirled in a firm circle over her clit.

On a long, low moan, she pressed her face back against his, enough that he could make out her expression. Eyes closed, she did look blissful, happy, trusting. And instead of that making him feel better, it suddenly made him feel like a fraud. Because he couldn't give her all of him, could he? He wouldn't reveal all of himself to her, would he? He shouldn't burden her with all the doubts and fears and uncertainties that had been building up inside him lately, should he?

Eyes tightly shut, he leaned his forehead against hers and concentrated on stroking her just like she liked it. He needed to give her this. At least this. If not everything she deserved.

She deserves better than you.

"Oh, God, I'm coming," she said, her hips surging. "Oh, God." Her body shuddered through the climax, and then she sighed on a long breath. "Wow. Appetizers rock."

Caden had to clear his throat to get his voice to sound half normal. "Yeah they do."

She chuckled and turned over, burying her face against his chest. They lay there for a long moment until she finally yawned. "I'm so tired."

"Me, too," Caden said, though probably not for the same reasons.

"Can we just fall asleep like this?" she mumbled.

"Anything you want," he said, wishing it was true. Because he wasn't dumb. A woman who wanted you to meet her family and who tattooed your initial onto her body wanted more. Maybe wanted everything. And he felt so amazingly privileged that Makenna James maybe wanted all that with him. But he also felt undeserving.

Always.

"I guess I gotta take care of the tattoo first," she said, pushing herself up. She stroked her fingers along the tribal tattoo on his calf. "Will you help me?"

"Of course," Caden said, scrubbing at the scar on the side of his head. "Be right there."

"Okay." She threw him a small smile over her shoulder before she got up. The light came on in the bathroom, sending a stream of brightness into the bedroom.

Which meant it was time to shake the fuck out of it. Because just like in that elevator, the darkness was only going to hide him for so long.

Nausea had Makenna tearing out of bed and dashing across the room. She threw up everything she'd had for dinner the previous night and possibly some stuff she'd eaten two weeks ago given how many times she wretched.

Damn. When she'd felt better yesterday, she'd assumed she was over the stomach virus. Maybe she ought to go to the doctor. Shuddering, she flushed the toilet, then pulled herself up to the sink to rinse out her mouth.

Which was when it occurred to her.

She was late.

No, she couldn't be—

There'd been that one time a condom broke as Caden pulled out, but Makenna had had a period since then. True, it had been light. But her periods had always been like that—light one month, heavier the next; coming twenty-eight days later one month, then thirty-one the next. Which was why she hadn't given the lateness much thought.

Except this nausea had her thinking.

No.

No.

Shit.

Thoughts reeling, she shuffled back into the bedroom, completely unsure what she was going to say, to find the bed empty. "Caden? Hey? Where'd you go?" She found the other rooms dark and empty. What the heck?

Flicking on the kitchen light, she found a note on the counter.

Red—

I didn't want to wake you. Realized I needed something from the house before my shift so I left early. Talk to you later. —C

Makenna frowned. In all the time that they'd been together, he'd never left before morning. On a sigh, she combed her fingers through her hair. Not that it meant anything. Oh, screw it, she was just out of sorts from her maybe-but-probably-not-bathroom-revelation. Back in the bedroom, she disconnected her phone from its charger and shot off a text.

Missed waking up to your freaking gorgeous face. Have a good day! xo

She didn't get a message right back, but he never texted while driving, and he was probably on his way to the station given the time. She sagged down onto the edge of the bed.

Could she really be pregnant? Her stomach did a flip flop that made her wrap her arms around herself. Crap. There was no way she could make it through the entire work day without finding out.

Forcing herself up, she threw on some leggings, a sweatshirt, and a pair of gray knit boots, and ran a brush through her hair. She bundled into her coat and grabbed her purse, and then she was a woman on a mission. This was one of the things she loved about where she lived—the little urban enclave of Clarendon had everything you could need, most of it within easy walking distance. Including the Walgreens, just two blocks away.

Soon she was standing in front of a shelf full of pregnancy tests. And, good God, why were there so many? Pluses, minuses, one line, two lines, words, symbols.

This is ridiculous. Right? I don't need these.

Except. Maybe I do?

Pull down your big girl panties and pee on a stick and you'll know for sure.

Right.

On a sigh, Makenna grabbed one test that claimed to be able to provide the earliest results. And then she picked another that not only gave the words "pregnant" or "not pregnant" but also estimated how many weeks had lapsed since her last ovulation. Awesome.

She made it back to her apartment in no time flat, and for the first time since she'd met Caden, she was glad he wasn't there. Only because she didn't want to burden him with a possible baby scare without knowing there was definitely something to worry about in the first place. If she thought he wasn't ready to hear *I love you*, she could only imagine that his unreadiness to hear *I'm pregnant* would probably have to be multiplied by a factor of, like, a gajillion.

Dumping the bag out into the bathroom sink, Makenna had the oddest thought—she didn't know what she wanted the results to say. Which made no sense given that she was twenty-five and they'd been together less than three months, but the thought was there all the same.

With her heart in her throat, she opened the boxes and laid the plastic sticks out in a row—two of each kind. She used them all, just to be quadruple sure. And then she waited. And her pulse raced. And her belly flipped.

And then the results came in.

Plus. Plus. Pregnant 3+. Pregnant 3+.

Makenna stared at the little windows like she was trying to decipher Sanskrit.

Plus. Plus. Pregnant 3+. Pregnant 3+.

She was pregnant. And it had been more than three weeks since she'd ovulated? How far along was she? She sank down onto the closed toilet lid and dropped her head into her hands.

Oh God. Ohgodohgodohgod.

Okay. Don't freak out.

Right. I'll do that right after I freaking freak out!

"Stop. Think this through," she said out loud. An idea came to mind and she went in search of her cell phone. She called her doctor's office and found out how to get a blood test—might as well start with confirming this.

She quickly showered and dressed for work so she could stop on the way to get the blood test and have a chance of getting the results back before the weekend. Because even though she knew—home pregnancy tests were way too accurate to get four false positives—she still wanted the official result. And she suspected Caden would, too.

Staring into the bathroom mirror, her gaze dropped to her stomach.

"I'm pregnant," she whispered to herself, as if she was revealing a secret. And she guessed she was. Because no way was she telling Caden until she knew everything there was to know.

CHAPTER ELEVEN

The nightmares were getting worse. They'd tormented him during the little bit of sleep he'd gotten the night before, so he'd gotten up and paced the living room, ultimately leaving rather than face Makenna's knowing eyes in the morning. And during the long period of no calls they'd had during today's shift, he'd drifted off, only for the nightmares to come at him again.

They all started the same.

It was the endings that were different.

In one, it was him and Makenna in the backseat when the car flipped, and it was Makenna who didn't survive while he did. He called her name over and over, but she never answered.

In another, Sean morphed into Makenna from an earlier version of the dream. It was her eyes that accused him. Her voice that said, "It shoulda been me. I shoulda been the one to live."

In a completely new spin of his subconscious, Caden became his father and Makenna, his mother. When the car flipped, Makenna suffered his mother's fate, her head battered against the side window, her neck breaking, her death instant. And not only was Caden trapped hanging upside down knowing that everything he'd ever loved was gone, but knowing, too, that it was his own fault.

He'd lost control. And she'd paid the price.

So by the time a call came in to the station, Caden's head was a fucking wreck. Which probably explained why he had his very first on-the-job panic attack while responding to the scene of an accident. It was the hair that did it. The female driver's long red hair.

His mind had done its usual thing, and for several long moments, he'd been absolutely sure his worst fears had come true. Makenna was dead in that car. His chest went tight, his breathing shallowed out, and he froze.

It didn't matter that Makenna rarely drove her car. Nor that the car in the accident hadn't been the same as Makenna's little Prius. Or that there was absolutely no reason why Makenna would be on Duke Street near Landmark Mall at four o'clock in the afternoon when she worked miles away in Roslyn.

His brain didn't trade in logic in moments like those.

Embarrassment aside, it was even worse that he could've jeopardized a patient's life. In the end, the woman's injuries weren't that serious. But that wasn't the point. He was fucking out of control, and he didn't know what the hell to do about it. He hadn't been this bad in years.

Then again, he hadn't had anything to lose in years, either.

Now he did. And *he* was losing it.

When they returned to the station house, his captain called him into his office.

Exhausted and strung out, Caden dropped into the chair in front of his captain's desk. In his forties and prematurely gray, Joe Flaherty had been Caden's supervisor all nine years he'd worked in this house, and he was aware of Caden's background. A few of the guys were too.

As a rule, Caden didn't flake out—he showed up early, he left late, he picked up extra shifts, he covered for the guys with families, he left his rig clean and well stocked, and he did the job to the best of his ability. They all knew he was solid. Well, until today.

"What happened out there, Grayson?" Joe asked, his voice concerned, but not unkind.

Caden scrubbed at his face. "I've been having trouble sleeping," Caden said. "Nightmares about the accident have been coming back lately for some reason." He shook his head, wanting to be honest, but not wanting to say more than he had to. He met Joe's gaze head on. "When I first saw the woman, I thought it was Makenna."

A thoughtful expression on his face, Joe nodded. "We all see someone we love in the face of a patient at some point, so don't beat yourself up about that," he said. "You talking to someone about the nightmares?"

He shook his head again. Caden hadn't sought any kind of therapy in years. He'd worked things out. Gotten himself under control. Learned ways to handle his shit.

Only, clearly, that wasn't all true anymore, was it?

"Maybe you need to consider it. Given your history, I always expected you to have issues responding to MVAs. The real miracle given the life-threatening nature of your accident and your PTSD is that you didn't. And I watched you."

Caden knew that was true. And he'd understood why. On some level, he'd actually appreciated it. Before his first times out there, he hadn't known how he might respond either. But he'd been so driven to repay the debt, to help how Talbot had helped him, that he'd never had an issue. Accident scenes had never been a trigger for him the way they could be for other crash survivors.

The accident had scarred him physically, but the emotional trauma stemmed from its consequences. From losing his family. From surviving what they hadn't. From being alone with their corpses—because he hadn't known until later that his father had actually lived. From being left alone, in the car and all the years after, when his father checked out on him. From the fact that it took so long for someone to come help him that he hadn't known they were real.

Caden nodded. "I hadn't realized things were getting to me as bad as they apparently are. I'll handle it."

Joe's eyes narrowed. "Don't try to go it on your own. If your PTSD is flaring up enough to cause nightmares and give you a panic attack, something is stressing you out. Go talk to someone. That's an order. Don't make me pull you off shifts."

A rock parked in his gut, Caden rubbed a hand over his scar. "Yeah. Okay."

"Now go home," Joe said. "Get some sleep. And ask Makenna when she's gonna bring around more of those chocolate-iced brownies."

"I'm still on," Caden said.

"And I'm telling you to cut out. C-Shift will be on soon, so we're covered. That wasn't a suggestion." Joe arched an eyebrow.

Well, fuck. Caden hadn't been sent home once in nine years. And even though nothing in Joe's tone or expression made him think there was anything punitive or even irritated about the command, Caden still felt he was letting down his captain, his station, his family—the only one he had.

This was the one place where he'd always had things together.

Standing took way more effort than he wanted to admit. He came to attention, spine straight, head up.

"Dismissed," Joe said.

Caden made quick work of going home—to his townhouse in Fairlington that was just three blocks away. Makenna wouldn't be at the apartment yet, and he was way too raw to be around her just then anyway.

Which was why he texted her a lie.

Came home sick. Flu or something. Gonna sleep it off here for a few days so I don't get you sick. Talk to you later.

He stared at the words for a moment, then he hit *Send*. Maybe it wasn't that much of a lie after all. Something *was* wrong with him. And he didn't want to burden her with it. At least not until he figured out what had happened, what it meant, and what he needed to do about it.

Makenna was going a little crazy. Sitting in a ball on her couch, she'd been flipping cable channels for fifteen minutes without seeing a single thing worth watching. How was that even possible? But that wasn't what was really driving her crazy.

No, she was going crazy because she hadn't seen Caden in three days. They'd been texting all weekend, but he was still sick and not wanting to make her sick. It was killing her not to go help him, but he kept insisting she not come.

On top of that, she was going crazy because she'd gotten the official results from her doctor, and they'd confirmed what she already knew. She was pregnant.

But they'd also told her something she hadn't known—based on her bloodwork, she could be as far along as eight weeks. Which meant it really had happened when that condom broke back in October. *Knowing* she was pregnant was the only thing keeping her from helping Caden whether he wanted her to or not. She probably shouldn't chance getting sick.

Given how far along she was, the doctor's office managed to fit her in for an ultrasound appointment for Tuesday. And part of what was making her crazy was not knowing whether she should tell Caden before Tuesday so he could go with her, or get the ultrasound by herself and make sure the baby was healthy before raising it with him. She knew she was probably overthinking the whole thing and not giving him enough credit, but all this alone time had hit at the worst possible moment and had her conjuring up every bad outcome possible.

And all the craziness was compounded by the fact that she didn't feel like she should tell anyone else *before* Caden. She'd resisted calling her best friend, Jen, who was out of town on a Christmas shopping trip with her mom anyway. Besides Jen, her other closest friends had been college roommates, none of whom lived in the D.C. area. At any rate, she wasn't so close with them anymore that she would've felt comfortable calling and dropping the *Hey, I'm pregnant and scared my boyfriend is going to freak out* conversation on them. In this moment, part of her wished she had more girlfriends, but she'd always had an easier time making guy friends. She'd always blamed that on growing up surrounded by men.

Which had her wondering what she was going to tell her family—and when. Patrick had always been a great sounding board for her. Because he was so much older than her, Ian, and Collin, he'd helped his dad out a lot when they were all young. Later, he became almost a mentor to Makenna as she made decisions about college and careers. And her dad had never been anything but incredibly supportive, even when she was the first in the family to move out of the Philadelphia area. But telling one James man could be akin to telling them all, and that definitely wasn't something she was ready to do yet.

Which was why at four o'clock on Sunday afternoon she was still in her pajamas and an entire pound bag of peanut M&Ms lay demolished on the end table next to her.

At least peanut M&Ms had protein.

Sorry lil' nut. I'll do better.

Makenna sighed.

And then she decided she'd had enough.

A woman on a mission, she turned off the TV and marched directly to the shower. Once clean, she awkwardly worked to apply Aquaphor to her tattoo, which had moved from being sore to being itchy. She threw on some comfortable clothes, stuffed her feet into boots, and grabbed her purse and coat. And then she headed to the store.

She had a care package to put together.

At the very least, she needed to *see* Caden, even if she didn't stay.

Thinking of what she liked to have when she didn't feel good, she roamed around the supermarket picking up chicken noodle soup and crackers, popsicles and ginger ale, tea bags for hot tea and bread for toast, among other things. As little as Caden had stayed there over the past two months, he couldn't possibly have much food in the house, which made her feel bad for not doing this sooner. She threw in pain medicine and throat lozenges and Pepto Bismol.

And then she passed the aisle full of holiday items. Gift wrap, decoration, candy, and toys made it look like the North Pole had exploded in the middle of the Giant. Makenna grabbed Caden a bag of peanut M&Ms, because he liked them, too. A shelf of stuffed animals caught her eye, and even though it was a little corny, she was drawn closer.

What said *Feel better!* more than a cuddly stuffed animal? The fact that she was considering giving it to a big, tattooed, pierced, and scarred guy made it kinda funny, too—and anything that might make him smile seemed like a good idea to her. Besides, Caden might look a little rough around the edges, but he was a big teddy bear inside. And she'd always loved that dichotomy about him.

And then she saw the perfect little guy.

He was a brown bear with black stitching here and there like he'd been hand-sewn or put back together. He had a sweet face and an even sweeter red patchwork heart on his chest. And something about all that stitchwork and the heart reminded her of Caden. Without letting herself overthink it, Makenna grabbed him and threw him in the cart.

It was a short trip from the store to Caden's townhouse. She'd always loved where he lived in Fairlington. Built in the 1940s to house workers for the then-new Pentagon office building, the neighborhood was all red-brick collections of townhouses grouped around small cul-de-sacs. They were charming and close to everything and some of the units were surprisingly spacious, including Caden's, which had two bedrooms and a finished basement.

As she parked her Prius in one of the visitors' spots, that got her to thinking.

Here she'd been wondering why he didn't get rid of *his* place. Given the baby, it would make much more sense for them to get rid of hers. Caden's house had easily twice the square footage of her apartment, and he didn't even use the room next to his bedroom, which would make a perfect nursery.

As she stared at the front of his house, her belly did a little flip. Obviously, she was getting ahead of herself. But thoughts of where the baby would live represented just one in about a million things she now had to consider. Well, they. *They* now had to consider. She had to stop thinking about this like she was on her own.

She had Caden.

And right now, he needed her.

Makenna collected all the bags from the car and hefted them up to his front porch. She had to sit some down to knock on the door.

It opened in less than a minute.

"Makenna? What are you doing here?" Caden asked, clearly surprised to see her. Wearing a pair of old sweatpants and a threadbare T-shirt, he was a sight for sore eyes, making her want to throw her arms around him and burrow into his chest. But he also had dark and almost sunken circles under his eyes like he hadn't slept in days, and something about his color wasn't quite right. He really did look unwell.

"I missed you too much to stay away anymore, so I brought you a care package. Well, it kinda grew into a care grocery order, but same difference." She smiled, though inside she was bursting to tell him their news. "I won't stay if you're not up to it, but at least let me put this away for you and maybe make you a bowl of soup or something." Was she imagining it, or did his face look thinner, too? God, she really should've come sooner.

He frowned but nodded, then reached down and grabbed the bags she'd rested on the porch. "You didn't have to do all this," he said, leading her inside. "But thank you."

"Of course, I did," she said as they walked through the open living and dining room to the small kitchen at the back of the house. "I've been dying to come take care of you, but I didn't want to wake you up if you were sleeping or something. But then I started worrying that you were over here needing help or food or medicine and would be too stubborn to ask for what you needed." She gave him a knowing smile.

He chuffed out a little laugh as they settled everything onto the counters. "Yeah. Well. You know me."

"So what's been going on? Is it a stomach virus? The flu?" she asked as she started unpacking the bags.

Brow furrowed, Caden crossed his arms and leaned against the counter. "Yeah. Uh, my stomach. But, it's starting to feel better." Looking down at the floor, he gave a little shrug.

And there was something so…almost…defeated in the gesture and his posture that Makenna immediately stopped what she was doing and went to him. "I don't care if you're sick. I'm hugging you." She gently wrapped her arms around his waist and held him. And damn if he didn't *feel* a little leaner, too. "Have you been getting sick a lot?"

Caden's arms came around her on a long sigh. Like he'd been needing her. "Nothing I can't handle," he said in a low voice.

Which probably meant he'd been puking his brains out. Poor guy. "You don't have to handle this on your own, you know. I would've come sooner. I would've slept over here to take care of you."

"Didn't want to be a burden." He nuzzled his face against her hair.

Heart clenching, she pulled back to look him in the eye. "Caden, you could *never* be a burden to me. No matter what you needed, I would be there for you. Every time. You can always count on that. Do you hear me?" How did he not know this by now? The question had her wanting to lay *all* her feelings on the line. If he knew she loved him, he'd know all of this was true. But she definitely wasn't doing that when he wasn't feeling good.

He stared at her a long moment, almost like he was weighing her words. Finally, he simply said, "Yeah." He kissed her forehead. "Thank you."

"Don't thank me. This is me officially taking care of you. Do you think you could eat something?"

"Probably," he said.

Makenna kissed his cheek, and his stubble tickled her lips. "This is kinda cute," she said, stroking her finger along the couple of days' worth of growth.

"Oh yeah?" He lips almost quirked into a smile. "Good to know."

"Yep," she said, returning to the groceries. She had everything unpacked within a few minutes. "What would you like?"

His gaze roamed over the choices. "Soup and crackers would be great." He stepped closer. "I can't believe you brought all this. Ooh, M&Ms." He picked up the bag.

Makenna laughed. "You might want to wait on those until you're not getting sick anymore. It would be a shame to ruin M&Ms by knowing what they look like when you vomit them."

"Nice," he said with a smirk.

"Just saying. Okay, you go sit, and I'll get everything ready," she said, shooing him from the kitchen. "Oh, wait. One other thing." She handed him the bag with the bear in it.

"What's this?" he asked.

"A feel-better present," she said, unable to hold back her grin. He was going to think this was so silly. And it was. In a good way.

Caden stuck his hand in and pulled out the stuffed animal. "You got me a teddy bear," he said, his face *finally* breaking into a little smile. He rubbed his hand over the scar on the side of his head, something she'd seen him do so many times.

"Everybody needs a teddy when they're sick," she said. "That's, like, totally common knowledge. He can keep you company when I'm not here." Which wouldn't be often, but still.

Nodding, Caden gave her the softest look. "Thanks, Red. I...I don't know what I'd do without you."

She smiled, so glad she'd come to see him. He needed this. They both did. "Well, don't worry about that. Because you won't ever have to find out."

CHAPTER TWELVE

Makenna walked alone into her doctor's office on Tuesday morning. After going back and forth, she'd decided the best approach was to gather all the information she could before telling Caden she was pregnant. Most importantly, she wanted to know that the baby was healthy. Assuming that was the case, she planned to tell him tonight after work. Tell him everything.

It was time. And she was bursting at the seams.

She checked in at the desk and took a seat. A number of other people were waiting, and two of the women were obviously pregnant. Excitement shivered through Makenna's chest. That was going to be her in not too many months. At the side of one of the women, a man sat whispering into her ear, making her laugh. He rested his hand on her belly as they spoke.

And that…that would be Caden. Who hadn't had a family in so very long. God, she hoped he was excited about having one now. Even if he was scared—hell, she was too—she hoped his excitement would outweigh it. Because at the end of all this, they were going to have a tiny product that was a part of them both. And that was amazing to Makenna.

The waiting room door opened. "Makenna James?" called a nurse wearing a set of pink scrubs.

She followed the woman to an exam room, her heart racing a little faster with each passing moment. Because she was about to see her child for the very first time.

Before too long, she was wearing a paper gown and her long-time gynecologist entered the room with a nurse. "Makenna, nice to see you again," Dr. Lyons said.

"Nice to see you, too," she said, smiling at the woman's always upbeat personality.

"Are you here alone today?" the doctor asked as she scrubbed her hands.

Makenna nodded. "I wanted to make sure the pregnancy was okay before telling my boyfriend."

"Okay," Dr. Lyons said, "well, let's get started then." The doctor explained how the internal ultrasound worked and then Makenna laid back with her feet in the stirrups—which always felt incredibly awkward no matter how many times she'd had to do it in her life.

But all of that fell away as an image appeared on the screen and a fast beat rung out in the room.

"Hello, little one," the doctor said, taking some measurements on the monitor.

Tha-thump tha-thump tha-thump tha-thump tha-thump.

"Is that the heart beat?" Makenna asked, the sound planting itself inside her chest and squeezing.

Dr. Lyons smiled as she made some adjustments with the ultrasound wand. "It sure is. Sounds perfectly normal, too."

"It's supposed to be that fast?" Makenna's gaze locked on the screen where the doctor had zooned in on a grainy, peanut-shaped object with tiny nubs protruding from the sides.

In her mind, she heard her father calling her *peanut*, and now she knew why.

That was her baby and he was totally a little peanut. Well, he or she.

"Based on the measurements here you're nine weeks and three days along, and your estimated due date is July seventh. Everything looks to be progressing normally." Dr. Lyons smiled. "So I think you're safe to share your news."

Makenna couldn't pull her gaze away from the screen. Suddenly, the whole situation crashed down on her and she caught her breath as tears pricked her eyes. "This is so incredible. I wish I'd brought him now."

"There will be plenty more to share with him, including more scans," the doctor said as she removed the wand. The image stayed on the screen. "And I'll send you away with parting gifts." The imagining machine made a *whirring* sound and spit out a strip of paper. Dr. Lyons handed it to her.

Pictures of their peanut. Makenna pressed them to her heart, any uncertainty she might've felt about having a baby disappearing. "I can't wait to show him. So everything's okay?"

"Yep. I want to put you on pre-natal vitamins and we'll get you set up with your pre-natal appointments. We'll see you back in four weeks." The doctor discussed some pregnancy dos and don'ts and gave her some information sheets to take home. God, there was a lot to learn about all this, wasn't there?

When they were done, the doctor walked to the door, then turned back with a smile. "Have fun telling your boyfriend tonight. I hope it goes great."

"Thanks," Makenna said. Dr. Lyons left, and Makenna slid off the table. Looking down at the pictures, she just felt so amazed and overwhelmed and excited. "I hope it goes great, too."

As Caden climbed the five flights of steps up to Makenna's apartment, he felt like years had passed since he'd last been there. He certainly felt like he'd *aged* years since he'd last been there.

What a wasted wreck he'd been the past few days. His PTSD hadn't flared like this for years. For most of the weekend, he hadn't slept, and when he had, the nightmares had been torturous. His mind was like a maze full of dark corners and dead-ends and looming shadows. He'd had no appetite, and the two times he'd tried to eat, he'd thrown it back up again. Luckily, Makenna had left on Sunday evening before he'd lost the soup and crackers she'd brought him. Aches racked his body like he really had been sick, and he'd had a non-stop headache since Friday night that made it hard to think.

All of which was why he was hoofing it up the steps. In the lobby, he'd stood in front of the open elevator door for a long moment before his central nervous system had threatened a full-on lock-down, and he'd known he just couldn't get in that little box. No matter how short a ride it would be. *That's* how out of control his bullshit was right now.

The last twenty-four hours had been his first shift back to work, and getting out of bed to get his ass down to the station had taken Herculean effort. Not to mention making it through the shift itself. It felt like he was walking through molasses-filled air that made his limbs heavy and his muscles tired.

He'd finally given in and made an appointment with his doctor.

As he stepped out into the fifth-floor hallway, Caden recalled feeling this bad once before.

When he'd been eighteen. During the weeks leading up to high school graduation, when he hadn't yet known exactly what he was going to do with his life but had at least known he couldn't keep living with his bitter shell of a father. The uncertainty of the situation and his father's near-total abdication of parental responsibility for or interest in Caden had been bad enough. But it was also what would've been Sean's sixteenth birthday, and the combination sent Caden into a downward spiral that had ultimately resulted in a diagnosis of depression.

And *fuck* if Caden wasn't feeling the similarities with that time more than he wanted to admit.

It felt like such a colossal defeat after having held himself together for so long. And now *everything* seemed to be coming apart at the seams.

It was all almost more than he could bear. And didn't that make him feel weak and worthless. He was better than this. He *should* be better than this. Sonofabitch.

He slid his key into the lock on the apartment door, eager to see Makenna. It had helped seeing her Sunday night, when she'd been so sweet as to bring him that care package. She was the light to Caden's darkness and had been since they'd been trapped in that elevator. If anyone could take some of the weight off his shoulders, if anyone could make it easier for him to breathe, it would be her.

Stepping into the apartment, he was instantly surrounded by the rich, spicy smell of tomato sauce, and for the first time in days, he actually felt hungry. "Red? I'm home," he called.

Makenna rushed out of her bedroom, wearing a pair of jeans and a blue sweater and the most beautiful smile. "There you are," she said, rushing right up to him. She flung her arms around his neck. "God, I've missed you."

"I missed you, too," he said, reveling in the press of her soft heat against all his cold hardness.

Loosening her hold, she pushed onto tiptoes and kissed him in a soft meeting of lips that quickly deepened to more. "Really missed you," she whispered.

Caden managed a little chuckle as he slid his hand into all that gorgeous red hair. "I can tell."

Makenna pulled back and gave him a smile. "Are you feeling better?"

He nodded, because what else was he going to do? And being with her did make him feel better, so it wasn't really a lie. "What smells so good?"

"I made spaghetti sauce and meatballs. All I have to do is cook the noodles and dinner will be ready. You hungry?"

"I could eat," he said. He'd kept down the small cup of corn chowder he'd eaten for lunch at the firehouse, so he was hopeful that his body would let him have this.

"Good," she said, slipping away to the stove. She turned on the burner under a big pot. "Make yourself comfortable. Everything will be ready in less than fifteen."

"Okay," he said, heading for the bedroom. He changed out of his uniform into a pair of jeans and a T-shirt, and then he sagged down to sit on the edge of the bed. Exhaustion settled over him like a lead blanket. God, what was wrong with him?

You know what's wrong, Grayson.

Yeah, he probably did. Goddamnit.

But for the next few hours, he was going to let all that go and just be with Makenna. If that was possible. He hauled himself off the bed and returned to the kitchen to help get dinner ready. Soon, they were seated at the table with mounding servings of spaghetti, sauce, and meatballs. Crusty, warm garlic bread filled a little basket, and Caden took a big piece for himself.

"This looks fantastic," he said.

"Good. Eat up. There's tons left," she said.

They dug in and ate in silence for a while—which was really unusual for Makenna. She'd always been the one initiating conversation or keeping it going. The talkative yin to his quiet yang.

Looking at her, he asked, "How was your day?"

"Oh." She looked up. Gave a little shrug and a nervous laugh. "The usual," she said, waving her fork.

Since he was the king of nervous awkwardness, he recognized it when he saw it. "Is everything okay?"

She scoffed. "Yeah. Of course." Her smile was just a watt too forced.

He arched an eyebrow and nailed her with a stare.

"Okay, fine," she said, setting her fork down. "I have some things I'd like to talk about, but I was trying to wait until we were done eating."

Caden didn't love the sound of that. He set his fork down, too. "What do you want to talk about?"

She heaved a deep breath, like she was bolstering herself for what she had to say. A boulder parked itself in his gut. "So, I have an idea. We've pretty much been living together for the last two-plus months, right?" He nodded, wariness clawing over his skin. "And I've been wondering why you're keeping your place because you're always here—which I love, but it's a waste of money, really. But when I was at your house the other night, it occurred to me that if we were going to think about fully moving in together, it would make more sense to move into your house since it's bigger. And then I'd get rid of this place." The words spilled out of her in a rush.

He stared at her for a long moment, his brain struggling to catch up, to process. "You want to move into the townhouse with me?"

"Well." Makenna gave a shy little shrug, one that revealed just how much she wanted it. "I've just been thinking about it."

Caden swallowed around a constriction in his throat. She wanted to move in together. Permanently. For a moment, it felt like maybe there wasn't enough air, but he forced a couple of deep breaths. The idea wasn't *that* big of a deal since they'd pretty much been living together. Right? Though, it took things to a whole other level. And it also took away his ability to retreat into his own space if he fell apart like he had this weekend. That realization sunk tension deep into his shoulders.

"Makes sense, I guess," he managed. "Let's think about it and decide what's best."

She twisted her lips. "Okay," she said. "It just doesn't seem to make as much sense to keep a smaller place when you have such a nice house right by where you work."

He braced his elbows on the table and clasped his hands together. And tried to ignore the pool of anxiety threatening to bubble up inside him. "Although it's further away from yours."

"True, but I don't mind," she said, her hands fidgeting on the table top.

"Well, like I said, let's think about it. Your place is a lot homier than mine."

Makenna smiled and waved a hand. "That's just because you haven't decorated much. But once we moved some of my furniture in and maybe did some painting and hung some pictures, your place would be homey, too. Your townhouse is great, Caden."

Tightness parked itself in the center of his chest. Why was she pushing on this right now? And why did it make him feel like the walls were closing in on him? "Okay," he said, picking up his plate and getting up from the table. "Dinner was great, by the way. Thank you." He walked into the kitchen, needing space so he didn't flip out when his stress really had nothing to do with her or her idea. He was just in a bad fucking place to be thinking about permanence, which made him feel like an asshole.

She followed him. "Gah, I'm going about this all wrong."

"Going about what?" he said, that rock getting a little bigger in his gut.

Makenna closed the distance between them, her hands falling on his chest, her baby blues looking up at him with so much affection. For a moment, she appeared to struggle for words, and then she said, "God, I'm being a tongue-tied idiot right now."

"Whatever you have to say, just say it," he said, dread prickling like ice all down his spine. Her unusual nervousness spiked the anxiety inside him and tightened the knot in his chest, making his breathing shallow out.

"Okay. Here goes. Caden, I…I love you. I love you so much that I can barely remember my life before you. I love you so much that I can't imagine my life without you. I've been dying to tell you, but I know we haven't been together that long. Though, to me, the number of weeks that I've known you feels completely meaningless to how attached my heart has become," she said, her voice urgent and so damn earnest. "I love you. And I'm *in* love with you. That's what I really wanted to say."

He heard the words as if through a long tunnel. They came to him slow and detached, as if his brain had to translate them from some other language to one he could understand, to one he could trust.

Makenna loved him.

Makenna had said the words. Words her actions had been communicating for weeks. Hell, maybe more.

The gates that held back the darkness in his psyche had been badly battered the past few days, and hearing her declaration destroyed what was left of them. All his fears, all his doubts, all his insecurities came rushing forth until he was drowning, suffocating, going under fast.

On the face of it, his reaction made no sense because she'd given him what he wanted—her love, her commitment. But it was getting what he wanted that made him so afraid.

Because deep inside, he was the fourteen-year-old boy who believed he should've died so his twelve-year-old brother—the best friend he'd ever had—could live. He was the kid sick with survivors' guilt who desperately wanted his father to acknowledge him instead of *choosing* to abandon him. He was a man who'd been taught that life didn't give you what you wanted, or if it did, it took it away again.

The past. Anxiety. Fucked-up fears. Caden knew it, but he couldn't fight it. His heart wasn't whole. His feet weren't steady. His brain wasn't right.

He wasn't right. And in that state, he didn't trust himself with loving her.

He grasped her hands and pulled them away from his chest. "Makenna, I—" But no further words came out, because it was like his brain had frozen. He knew what he felt, but he didn't know what to say. How to put it into words, or whether he even should. He was fucking paralyzed.

"You don't have to say it back," she said, something sad and maybe even a little disappointed flashing through her eyes. "I didn't say it with an expectation that you would say it back."

So she'd expected him to fail her. And that's what he was doing. Like he needed more proof that she deserved better.

He gasped a breath, all the stress of the past week crashing down on him like a ton of bricks. Or maybe it was more like a house of cards, because in this moment Caden felt like a fucking fool to have ever believed that he was capable of being one of two when his half of that equation was so damn damaged.

"Makenna, it's just, this is all…" Shaking his head, he stepped back, out of her grasp. His skin was suddenly too sensitive to allow her touch. Hell, the clothes on his back felt too rough, too heavy, too confining. "It's just a lot. It's just fast," he said, not even sure of the words coming out of his mouth.

A look of hurt flashed across her pretty face, and even though she tried to hide it, tried to recover, he knew what he'd seen. "It doesn't have to mean anything—"

"Yes, it does," he bit out, hating that his emotional bullshit was making her discount her feelings. To try to make him feel better. "It means fucking everything." He grasped at his chest, the lack of oxygen setting off a burn right in the center. His head throbbed out a punishing downbeat.

"Caden—"

"I'm sorry," he said, wincing as he tried to suck in a deep breath. "I can't...I gotta...go. I just need some space. Okay? Some time?" His fight or flight instinct was kicking him in the ass. Hard. "I...just need some space. I'm sorry."

Then he was out the door, his whole world imploding around him. Because he'd probably just destroyed the best thing he'd ever had. But maybe that was as it should be, since he clearly couldn't handle it anyway.

And Makenna deserved someone who could.

CHAPTER THIRTEEN

Makenna stared at her apartment door, the sound of it closing still echoing loudly all around her. What the hell just happened?

She clutched her stomach, just that moment realizing she'd never even gotten to the point of telling Caden about the baby. And, Christ, how was she supposed to do that now? When hearing that she loved him sent him into a full-out panic attack. Never in all the time she'd known him had she ever seen his face go so pale and distant and just…blank out like that. Like she was looking at a shell of the man she knew.

Given how marked by abandonment he was, she'd always worried that hearing her say she loved him might trigger his anxiety. But she never thought it would be this bad.

On instinct, she dashed for the door and wrenched it open, but the hall was empty. She sagged against the door jamb and stared at the emptiness.

Every urge within her told her to run after him. But he'd asked for time and space. Would going after him make things worse? Would it push him away? Was it worth the risk?

The thing was, Makenna understood a lot about how Caden reacted to things. And, after doing some reading on the subject, she understood a lot about how his anxiety and PTSD worked—that didn't mean she always knew how to handle it, and she certainly had no imaginings that she could fix it, but she understood that he faced these struggles. Hell, his need for a distraction from his claustrophobia and anxiety was what had led them to get to know each other in the first place.

And she didn't love him *despite* of all of his issues, she loved him *because* of them. Or, rather, because they were part of who he was. And she loved who he was. With everything she had.

Which meant she should probably give him the space he needed. Even if it left her heart an aching, bruised mess.

She walked back into her kitchen and let the door fall closed behind her.

Dropping her head into her hands, Makenna fought back tears. She'd gone about that conversation all wrong. At the table, she'd gotten nervous about the big things she had to tell him so she'd blundered into the conversation about moving in together. Which no doubt must've seemed to Caden like it came from out of left field. And then she'd piled on her feelings.

"Okay, don't panic," she said to herself. Her words sounding loud in the quiet space. "He'll be fine. We'll be fine." She just had to keep telling herself that for however long he needed.

Desperate to keep busy, she mechanically worked through putting the sauce and meatballs into bowls for lunch and to freeze, and then she dove into doing the dishes.

When she was done, she gave in to the yearning inside her and sent Caden just one text:

Take as much time and space as you need. I'll be here no matter how long that is. xo

She hit *Send* and then went to bed, hoping against hope that he'd feel better in the morning.

But the morning didn't bring any word from Caden. Nor did the afternoon, or the next night. Or any day that week. By Friday night, Makenna was a wreck of worry and heartache. She couldn't bring herself to go home and face her empty apartment. She was worried for him that he was in such a bad place, and she was worried for herself that it might be so bad he'd never make his way back to her.

And she didn't know what to do.

So she went back to her apartment building to get her car. She wasn't sure where she was going or what she was even thinking. Or maybe that was just kidding herself. Because within twenty-five minutes, she was driving down Caden's street, and then past his small cul-de-sac. She slowed down enough to see that his place was dark and his Jeep wasn't parked in its usual spot. So next she made her way to the Station 7 Firehouse just a few blocks away.

His Jeep wasn't there either.

Her car idling along the curb on the far side of the street, Makenna stared at the building, a golden glow spilling out into the street from some of the windows.

Part of her was sorely tempted to go in and see if any of the guys knew where she might find him. Or at least knew how he was. Had he even been going to work? But another part of her worried that going to his job to ask after him was crossing a line. Certainly a line that violated his request for space, and possibly one that could impact his livelihood.

She couldn't bring herself to do it…but maybe she could call one of the guys she'd gotten to know a little better. Isaac Barrett! He'd come to her house one night for dinner with Caden and a few of the other guys, he'd often made a point of talking to her when she'd come out to the station's softball games earlier in the fall, and he'd given her a big hug when she'd dropped cookies and brownies off at the firehouse. She wouldn't call them close, but maybe close enough to ask a couple hopefully casual-sounding questions.

Luckily, she had his cell phone number from when he'd RSVP'd for that dinner. She found it in her contacts and pressed *Send*.

Two rings, then, "Hello? Bear here."

"Bear, it's Makenna James, Caden's—" She momentarily got tripped up on what to call herself given what was going on between them. "—uh, girlfriend."

"Makenna of the wonderful brownies," he said. "To what do I owe this pleasure?"

"Hey, I'm sorry to bother you but I was wondering if you might know where Caden is." There. That sounded casual. Right?

"Gimme a second," he said. Muffled words she couldn't make out sounded in the background, and then a door closed. "I'm back. So, Caden took a leave of absence. Didn't you know?"

A leave of absence? Makenna's belly slowly sank as a feeling of dread spread through her. Caden was so dedicated to his job, so much so that it seemed more like a calling to him. She couldn't imagine him walking away from it. Unless he absolutely had to. "Unfortunately, no."

"Is he okay, Makenna?" Bear asked. "His last coupla shifts, he was running way ragged."

"He'd been sick," she said. "But, I don't know, maybe there's something else."

"Yeah," Bear said in a knowing voice. "I hope everything's okay."

"So do I," she said, her throat suddenly thick with tears. "If you hear from him, is there any chance you'd let me know? I'm…well, I'm worried."

"Count on it," Bear said. They hung up.

Sitting in her car in the darkness, Makenna finally gave into the tears she'd been holding back all week.

His Jeep parked in a spot behind Makenna's building, Caden didn't know what he was doing there. His head and his heart were still a fucked-up wreck, and he had no idea what he'd even say if he saw her. He had no more clarity, no more certainty, no more faith in himself than when he'd left there Tuesday night. And the last thing he wanted to do was hurt her more than he'd undoubtedly already done.

All he knew was that he'd been drifting through life for days—more ghost than human—until he'd finally gravitated there.

Like she was the sun to his dark planet.

Not at all sure he was doing the right thing—for her—he hauled his ass out of the Jeep and made his way to her place. By the stairs again, *offuckingcourse*.

His head had gotten so bad that he'd not only admitted just how bad to his captain, but he'd taken a leave of absence. For the first time in nine years of doing this job, he didn't feel that he was fully competent, and the last thing he wanted was to make a mistake that would cost someone everything. He wouldn't be able to live with that.

And he was holding on by a very thin string.

He'd also given in and gone to the doctor for meds, and even went back to see his old therapist. Dr. Ward was in his late forties now, and his hair was a little grayer and his waistline a little wider, but otherwise, he looked pretty much like Caden remembered.

So far, Caden had only had one session with the guy, and it had worsened his nightmares. Talking had always been like that for him—stirring shit up so that it got worse before it got better. But he had to try something. Because feeling like this wasn't tenable.

When Caden got to the apartment door, he knocked. Waited. Knocked again. He had a key, of course, but given how he'd left things on Tuesday night, he thought he owed her the respect of knocking. When she still didn't answer after knocking a third time, he let himself in.

Everything was quiet and dark—only the under-counter lamp in the kitchen threw off any light.

Caden heaved a deep breath. An ache ballooned inside his chest. An ache for Makenna. He missed her something fierce. It felt like a part of himself had been ripped away, the edges still jagged and raw.

But that's what he was—all jagged, raw, festering wounds from one loss after another.

And it didn't seem like a single one of them had healed.

He wandered through the darkness and into her bedroom. He sat down on the bed. Makenna's scent was stronger here. Her vanilla skin lotion. Her strawberry shampoo. The coconut hand cream she rubbed on before bed each night. He breathed those hints of her in, needing to carry some small part of her with him.

Knock, knock, knock.

Frowning, Caden forced himself up and to the front door. A quick peak through the spyhole revealed a delivery man of some sort. Caden opened the door.

"Makenna James?" the delivery man said. At his feet sat a huge vase of red roses.

"She's not home," Caden said, staring at the flowers.

"Would you please sign for me then, sir?" He thrust a clipboard at Caden, who scrawled an unintelligible line at the X. The guy retreated down the hall.

Caden bent down and grasped the crystal vase. Carried it to the kitchen counter, the door slamming closed behind him. Placed it down. And stared some more—at the little envelope sitting among the fat, red blooms.

With a sinking feeling in his gut, he pulled the envelope free and opened it. The card read:

Take as much time as you need. I'll be here. And I love you. ~CH

CH. Cameron Hollander. Sonofafuckingbitch.

Without returning the card to the envelope, Caden slipped both back into the plastic holder, his gaze glued to the other man's words.

Caden hadn't been able to deal with Makenna saying she loved him and hadn't been able to give her the words back, yet here was Cameron giving them to her again and again. Which was exactly what Makenna deserved.

Jesus Christ. Hands braced against the counter, Caden found himself having to breathe through a sudden clenching tightness in his chest.

Makenna deserved…someone like Cameron. Someone whole, someone unbroken, someone with his shit together. Caden was not that man. Hell, right now, Caden wasn't even the man Makenna had met in that damn elevator. At best, he was a ghost of his former self, and that guy hadn't even been fully squared away.

Maybe Makenna didn't want Cameron like she once did, but she deserved someone who could do what Cameron could—and what Caden couldn't.

And that was all Caden needed to know.

Disappointment and frustration and sadness and anger whirled inside him. He forced himself away from those fucking flowers before he hurled them across the room just for the satisfaction of seeing them shattered and broken—a mirror of how he felt inside.

Not quite sure what he was doing, he stalked back to the bedroom. Flicked on the light. Stood there. On the nightstand next to his side of the bed lay a military thriller he'd been reading a few pages at a time before going to sleep.

He grabbed it.

Suddenly, he was grabbing everything of his that was there. Uniforms. Clothes. Shoes. Toiletries. He didn't deserve to be in Makenna's life, not when he couldn't give her what she needed, what she wanted, and what she deserved. He had to do the right thing. For her.

His chest in a vise, he stuffed all of his belongings into a black trash bag.

Standing in the middle of the kitchen, he stared at the fucking flowers one last time. And then he left a note—and his apartment key—on the counter beside them.

CHAPTER FOURTEEN

A little after ten o'clock, Makenna finally made her way home. After leaving the firehouse, she'd driven to her favorite Mexican restaurant and had dinner sitting at the bar—a table for one just feeling more depressing than she could stand. Next, she'd gone to the bookstore for a while, but finally left when she realized she was browsing the bargain books for thrillers Caden might like.

Opening the apartment door, the first thing she noticed was that the overhead kitchen light was on. As was her bedroom light. "Caden?" Her heart swelled inside her chest as an ocean of sheer relief rushed through her. "Caden?" she called again as she hurried back to the bedroom.

But the place was empty.

She returned to the kitchen. Because the second thing she'd noticed was a huge vase of roses sitting on the counter. Among the blooms, she could just make out the words, *I love you. ~C*

"Oh, God," she said, her throat going tight. Caden had been there. He'd come to tell her he loved her. And all the while she'd been avoiding coming home.

Makenna pulled the card from the plastic holder. And her stomach dropped to the floor.

Take as much time as you need. I'll be here. And I love you. ~CH

CH. Freaking Cameron. Crap.

Makenna's shoulders sagged. Not Caden. Not Caden, after all.

And then she noticed something else.

A note next to the vase. Dread skittered over her skin as she lifted and read it.

You may not want him, but you deserve more than me.

It wasn't signed, but she didn't need it to be. Makenna recognized Caden's handwriting. And beneath the note lay his apartment key.

Caden *had* been there.

She frowned, her thoughts racing. *You deserve more than me?* What did that even mean? And why did he relate it to Cameron, whose card he'd obviously opened and read? And why had he left his key?

Dread wrapped around her now like a second skin. Caden's note and key clutched tightly in her hand, she walked back to the bedroom. Slowly, tentatively, like something might jump out at her. She wasn't sure what she was looking for as she stepped into the room. Everything looked the same as when she'd left this morning.

Then Makenna walked into the bathroom. It only took a split second for her to notice what was different. Her toiletries were the only ones on the counter. His toothbrush, toothpaste, and razor were gone. She opened the medicine cabinet. His floss, mouthwash, and shaving cream were gone. Pulling back the shower curtain revealed that his body wash was no longer there.

A raw ache settled into her chest. "No," she said, rushing into the bedroom again. "No, no, no." She flung open the walk-in closet door. Caden was a pretty basic guy when it came to clothes. A few pair of jeans, a few shirts, his uniforms. So he'd never taken up much space in her closet. But what space his things had taken was now vacated. His clothes and shoes were gone.

"No, Caden, no," she said, tears straining her voice. *Don't give up. Don't give up on us.* "Damnit."

Makenna raced back to the kitchen and fished her cell from her purse. She called Caden. Again and again it went to voicemail until she finally gave in and left a message. "Caden, please talk to me. What's going on? I don't understand. I'm here for you. Please just let me in. Whatever it is, we can fix it." She debated for a long moment, and then she added, "I love you."

She pressed *End* and hugged the phone to her chest.

Numbness settled over her. Numbness and denial.

Without getting changed, she laid down on her bed, phone in hand. *Call me. Call me. Call me.*

The next time she opened her eyes, the first gray light of day spilled through her windows. She woke up her phone to see she hadn't missed any calls or texts.

He'd packed up and walked out of her life, and he wasn't returning her messages.

As Makenna lay there in the darkness, she couldn't help but face the truth of what was happening. What *had* happened. Caden had left her because he thought she deserved something more than him. Caden had left her because he didn't think he was enough for her. How many times had he said something along those lines? And he was still saying it, despite the fact that she'd told him she loved him, that she was *in love* with him, and that she couldn't imagine her life without him.

If those sentiments weren't enough to make him believe that she wanted him—wanted *them*—she didn't know what else she could possibly say or do to convince him.

Makenna's numbness wore off in a cold rush.

Pain lanced through her blood until she was consumed by it. Her heart. Her head. Her soul. Curling into a ball, she sobbed into her pillow. She cried for herself. She cried for Caden. She cried for what they'd been—and everything they could've been still.

And then she thought of the baby—and of the fact that Caden didn't even know it existed—and she cried for the little life they'd made, too.

What was she going to do?

What were *they* going to do? Her and the baby.

She didn't know. Not yet. But she was going to have to figure it out. She was going to have to be strong for her son or daughter. And for herself.

And she would. But today she was going to let herself grieve. Because it wasn't every day that she lost the love of her life.

CHAPTER FIFTEEN

All weekend, every time Caden woke up, he played Makenna's voicemail.

Caden, please talk to me. What's going on? I don't understand. I'm here for you. Please just let me in. Whatever it is, we can fix it. Pause. *I love you.*

He dragged the little arrow backward with his thumb. *I love you.*

And again. *I love you.*

And again. *I love you.*

CHAPTER SIXTEEN

Caden couldn't do anything but sleep. Even though nightmares tormented him. Even though his muscles ached from lack of use. Even though life passed him by.

Although that hardly seemed to matter. Ghosts weren't alive anyway.

Every so often, he got up long enough to take a piss, choke down his meds, and stare aimlessly into his refrigerator. Sometimes he ate. Sometimes he watched television.

But then his thoughts and his fears and his failures became too painful to endure.

So he went back to bed.

CHAPTER SEVENTEEN

The banging wouldn't fucking stop.

At first Caden thought it was his head, which would've been par for the goddamned course, but then he heard someone shouting his name. Over and over and fucking over.

Dragging himself from bed was an effort he barely had the energy to make. He shuffled out of his room and down the steps, his legs feeling weak, his muscles aching from disuse.

He looked through the spyhole. "Fuck," he bit out.

"I'm not leaving until you open this door," his captain yelled. "I'll break it down if I have to."

Pound, pound, pound.

Caden knew Joe Flaherty enough to know he was good to his word. And that he'd broken down more than one door in his career as a firefighter.

Kicking aside the big pile of mail that had collected on the floor under the mail slot, Caden unlocked and opened the door, just a little. "Captain. What can I do for you?"

"Let me the hell in," Joe said, pushing the door open further and stepping in to Caden's living room. "Jesus fucking Christ, Grayson." The older man stared at him, his expression shocked.

Caden looked down at himself, at his bare chest and stomach and the dark gray sweatpants hanging loosely on his hips. "What?"

Joe's eyes widened. "What? *What?* Are you telling me you don't know you're a goddamned skeleton?" He raked his hand through his graying hair. "I called. Over and over. But I knew I should've come sooner."

Confused, Caden shook his head. "I don't…I'm sorry…what—"

"Do you have any idea what day it is?" Joe asked, hands planted on his hips.

Caden thought about it. And thought some more. He tried to remember the last time he knew what day it was. He'd left Makenna's on a Friday. And then slept for days. He'd tried to get up for an appointment with his therapist, but hadn't been up to it. That had been on a…Thursday? And he'd been up some other times for a bite to eat or to stare mindlessly at the television. But…uh, no. He had no idea. Rubbing his hand over his scar, he shrugged.

Joe turned on the lamp beside the couch and sat heavily. "Sit down, Caden."

Frowning, Caden shuffled to the couch. Sat. Braced his elbows on his knees. God, his head was heavy.

"What's going on?" Joe asked, his face a mask of concern.

Caden shook his head. "Nothing."

The other man's expression slid into a scowl. "Do I need to take you to the emergency room? Because I will haul your ass out of here in a heartbeat—"

"What? No." Caden scrubbed his hands over his face. "I know I'm off right now, but I'm...I'll..." He shrugged again, not knowing what to say. He'd walked out on Makenna mid-spiral and hadn't been able to do anything but hold on until he hit bottom. Was he there yet? Hell if he knew. Although he could hardly imagine feeling much worse than he did just then. Physically, emotionally, mentally.

Everything fucking *hurt*, like he was agony personified.

"You're off? You're not off, Caden. You're clinically depressed, if I had to guess. And looking at you, I really don't need to do that. What have you lost? Twenty pounds? Thirty? Jesus. When was the last time you ate?"

"I...I don't...I can't keep anything down." Caden dropped his gaze to the floor. "But I'm not hungry anyway."

"Of course you're not. That's the depression. Fuck, I'm sorry I didn't come sooner. I should've known..." Joe heaved a breath. "How bad is it?"

Caden kept his eyes down. Really bad. Way worse than it'd been when he was eighteen. Or maybe he was misremembering just how empty and painful and isolating and pointless and worthless depression had previously made him feel. "Bad," he said, his voice little more than a whisper.

"Thoughts of hurting yourself bad?" Joe asked.

Humiliation roiling through his gut, Caden couldn't look Joe in the eye. Yeah, he had those thoughts. The ones that sometimes taunted him with the promise of freedom from all this fucking misery. He hadn't considered them seriously, but he couldn't deny having them.

"Shit. Okay. What are we going to do about this?"

"We?" Caden's gaze cut to his captain.

"Yeah, *we*. You think I'm leaving you alone like this? You're coming to my house today, and tomorrow you're either going to your doctor or to the hospital. And I'm taking your ass. And I'll keep taking you until you get this under control. In fact, I'll help you pack a bag. You're staying with me until we turn this thing around." Joe arched a brow and nailed him with a stare.

"Cap—"

"None of that's up for discussion, Grayson. In case that isn't clear." Joe glared at him, but it was a glare Caden had seen many times before, when something hadn't gone quite right on a call— one born of concern, and maybe even a little fear.

"Okay," Caden said, too tired to fight the man. "I got meds, but I've missed some."

"Did you take one today?" Joe asked. Caden shook his head. "Then do it. How long have you been on them?"

He'd gone back to his therapist the day before he'd walked out of Makenna's life. "The tenth, I think it was."

Joe nodded. "Good. That's good. Even if you've missed some, that's two weeks' worth of medicine. Fucking shame antidepressants take so long to build up in your system. But at least you have a jump on it."

"Wait," Caden said, frowning. "Two weeks?" His eyes went wide. "Shit. What day is it?" His leave of absence ended on the twenty-third so he could take shifts to let the guys with families have the Christmas holidays off.

His captain clasped him on the back of the neck and gave him a look filled with so much compassion that Caden actually got a little choked up. "It's Christmas, Caden."

Christmas? *Christmas?*

"Fuck," he said, shoving into a standing position. Adrenaline punched through his system, leaving him wired and wobbly. "I…I'm sorry…*fuck*…I can't believe…I missed…everything."

"Don't give it a second thought. That's how I knew something was wrong," Joe said, standing up beside him. "You've never missed a day of work in almost ten years until all this happened. And then Bear told me that Makenna had called a few weeks ago because she didn't know where you were. Knowing you'd checked out on work *and* her, I knew something was wrong."

Makenna.

Hearing her name out loud was like a punch to the gut. Caden pressed his fist against the jagged throb in his chest.

Makenna.

The sob came out of nowhere.

Caden slapped his hand over his mouth, horrified to fall apart in front of Joe, to show him just how weak he really was.

But it was like her name unlocked something inside him, and it felt like whatever it was had been the very last thing holding him together. "Fuck," Caden choked out, falling heavily to the couch. He dropped his face into his hands, a vain effort to hide the unhideable. His tears. His sobs. His grief.

His failure.

Joe was right there with him. Hand on his shoulder, the man sat beside him. "It'll get better. Just hang on. We'll get you through this."

When Caden could manage to talk again, he shook his head. "She's gone," he rasped, sliding his wet hands to cradle his throbbing forehead. "I...I fucked everything up."

"Don't worry about that. Worry about you. Fix you. Then you can work on whatever else you want. But it starts with you." Joe squeezed his shoulder. "And I'll be here to help."

Caden tilted his head to the side just enough to see Joe's face. "Why?"

His captain nailed him with a stare. "You really gotta ask?"

"Yeah," he rasped.

"Because you're a great part of my team, Caden. Excellent at what you do. More than that, after all these years, I consider you a friend. And if all that wasn't enough, you're a good fucking human being, and I'm not losing you to whatever bullshit lies your head is telling you. I know you don't have any family, so I'm officially stepping in and stepping up. I will fight for you until you can fight for yourself. You hear me?"

The words reached inside Caden's chest...and eased him. Not a lot. Not permanently. But enough to take a deep breath. Enough to let his shoulders loosen. Enough to begin to think beyond the next five minutes.

Caden respected the hell out of Joe Flaherty. Had for his entire adult life. And if Joe believed all that about Caden, maybe there was truth in what he said. And if Joe was willing to fight for Caden, maybe Caden could figure out how to fight for himself, too.

It starts with you.

That idea connected to something deep inside Caden. He didn't know what it was. He didn't know what it meant. But he grasped onto it, and he grasped onto Joe's support. Because he had to grasp on to something.

Before he lost himself forever.

CHAPTER EIGHTEEN

Makenna pulled her car into her father's driveway, her stomach a nervous, nauseous wreck. For once, that wasn't her morning sickness talking. It was the looming conversation she needed to have with her dad and brothers. The one that informed them she was pregnant and nearly twelve weeks along. And that the father was out of the picture.

Two weeks had passed since Caden had left his key. Two weeks since she'd left that voicemail. Two weeks of silence, although she had sent him a Christmas card. One last attempt to reach out.

No. Don't think about Caden.

Heaving a deep breath, she nodded to herself. She couldn't think of him without getting upset. And angry. And confused. And worried. None of which made her love him any less, though, which just made her so, so sad.

Enough. It's Christmas.

Right. It would've been their first.

The thought made her eyes sting.

She forced her gaze to the ceiling of her car, pinching off the threatening tears.

When she'd reined herself in, she retrieved the shopping bags of gifts from her back seat and made her way inside.

"There's my peanut," Dad said when she walked into the kitchen, the nickname making her throat tight. The smell of pancakes and bacon surrounded her—Dad had made the same thing for Christmas breakfast every year since forever.

"Hi," she managed. "Merry Christmas."

Patrick sat at the breakfast bar, the newspaper spread out in front of him and a coffee mug in his hand. "Merry Christmas," he said, an affectionate smile on his face. "Wondering when you were gonna get here."

"I know," she said, guilt eating at her. She'd never missed a Christmas Eve at home before, but the holiday had really hit her hard the day before and she'd just needed the time to herself. So she'd called and blamed her inability to make the trip on a bad headache. "I'm sorry I didn't make it yesterday."

"Feeling better?" her dad asked. She nodded. He wiped his hands on a tea towel and took her bags. "Let me help with these," he said, carrying them into the living room for her. She followed him in and was just about to comment on how pretty the Christmas tree looked when he turned with his arms wide open.

Swallowing the words, Makenna fell into his embrace, needing it like she hadn't needed a hug from her father in years. Needing the support and the protection and the unconditional love she'd always found in this man, who'd managed to give her and her brothers everything they needed in a family, even though they'd all lost their mother.

"Merry Christmas, Daddy," she said.

"It is now that all my kids are home." He put his arm around her shoulders and led her into the kitchen. "Hungry?"

"Famished, actually," and she was. Being here was good. Being here helped. It beat back the loneliness she'd been battling. It proved she wasn't alone, no matter what. It distracted her from her troubles. And it reminded her that, as much as she'd lost, she had so very much to be grateful for, too.

"Where are Collin and Ian?" she asked, bumping her shoulder against Patrick's. He pulled her into a one-armed hug.

"They were getting cleaned up. Should be down any minute," her dad said as he poured a few circles of batter onto the griddle.

"How's Caden? What's he doing today?" Patrick asked.

Makenna was prepared for this one. "Since he had Thanksgiving off, he had to work Christmas." At least that's what he'd said back at Thanksgiving. She wasn't sure if he was back to work or not. She hadn't let herself call Bear again, and he hadn't called her.

Patrick nodded. "I hear that. I'm on tonight, but at least I have the day."

Footsteps on the stairs sounded out, and then Collin and Ian joined them in the kitchen. Another round of hugs and greetings and Christmas wishes ensued.

"How are you feeling?" Makenna asked Collin. His hair had grown in enough to begin to cover the scar on the side of his forehead.

"Doing okay. Still having some headaches, but it's better than it was," he said. "I wish Caden had come. I would've liked to thank him for everything he did while I was actually with it."

Makenna hugged herself and forced a smile. "You did thank him. Anyway, he'd tell you he was just doing his job."

"Still," her father said, pointing with his spatula, "he made a bad night better. Him and Patrick both. I'll never forget that."

A knot of emotion lodged in Makenna's throat. "Can I have blueberries in my pancakes, Dad?"

"Heck, yeah. Blueberries, chocolate chips, M&Ms, whatever you kids want," her dad said with a laugh.

That set off a flurry of conversation about the pancakes that thankfully got them off of talking about Caden. Makenna ducked her head into the fridge as she looked for the blueberries and the strawberries Collin wanted.

Christmas breakfast was its usual fun and rowdy affair. They talked, joked, laughed. Her dad told stories from when they were kids, including a few about their mom. That was part of their tradition. Their mother might not be with them anymore, but she was still a part of them. Her dad made sure of it.

And that was the moment it really hit Makenna that her baby was going to grow up without a parent just like she had.

She made a quick excuse and slipped away from the table, hoping her exit hadn't appeared as hurried as it felt. She made a beeline for the hall bathroom and locked herself inside. And damn if her first thought wasn't about the time she'd locked her and Caden inside the very same room so she could talk to him about Cameron.

She sagged back against the door, silent tears rolling down her face. She fought against them, knowing if she let the flood gates open she might not be able to close them again. Her quiet sniffles and shuddered breaths filled the room.

Maybe the baby wouldn't grow up without one of his parents. Maybe once she told Caden about the baby, he'd at least want to be involved in the kid's life.

Because she absolutely had to tell Caden. She knew that. And she planned to do it. The question was when. She hadn't told him yet because she'd been hoping he'd realize he made a mistake and come back to her—and if he did, she wanted it to be for *them*. Makenna and Caden. *Not* because she was pregnant with his baby.

So, at some point, she was going to have to talk to him again. To see him. At the very least, she wanted to give Caden the opportunity to see the baby during her next ultrasound. He deserved that. He deserved to be involved, to know his child.

That appointment wasn't for another six weeks, but Makenna was already excited because it was the one where she could learn the baby's sex. She'd already decided that she wanted to know. For some reason, when she thought about the baby, she always thought of him as a boy. Maternal instinct or pure randomness? She'd find out soon.

Pull it together, Makenna.

Right.

She cleaned up her face and took a deep breath, then walked out the door.

And nearly walked into Patrick, standing in the hallway. Arms crossed. Clearly waiting. "Wanna tell me what's wrong?" he asked.

Leave it to Patrick to realize something was wrong. "Nothing," she said, giving him a smile.

He arched an eyebrow, his frown deepening.

Makenna sighed. "Later."

"Promise?" he asked. She nodded, and he pulled her into his arms. "Whatever it is, I'm here for you."

A quick nod against his chest, and then she pulled away. "Come on. It's time for presents."

Later came faster than Makenna hoped. Certainly faster than she was prepared for. Though, honestly, there was really no way to prepare for what she had to tell her family.

They'd exchanged presents. Watched *A Christmas Story*—because it really wasn't Christmas without Ralphie wanting a BB gun and shooting his eye out. Helped their dad make their traditional beef tenderloin dinner. And now that they'd eaten and dinner was all cleaned up, Patrick kept giving her that eyebrow.

If she didn't say something, he would.

"Can we all sit in the living room for a minute? I need to tell you guys something," Makenna finally said, her belly flipping.

"Is everything okay?" her dad asked, coming around the kitchen island to her.

"Yeah, but, can we just go sit down?" she asked.

The guys all gave her strange looks, but everyone followed her in and took seats around the room, Dad and Patrick on either side of her on the couch. The Christmas tree stood in front of the big window and threw off a multi-colored glow from the hundreds of lights strung through its branches. She'd missed decorating it yesterday, the day the James family had decorated its tree for as long as she could remember.

"What is it, Makenna?" her dad asked.

Makenna's heart thundered against her breastbone and a tingly nervousness fluttered through her. "So, I have some news."

Beside her, Patrick heaved a deep breath.

She met his gaze, and then her dad's, and then Collin's and Ian's. "I'm pregnant." Makenna nearly held her breath waiting for their reaction.

For a moment, no one said a thing, and then her father moved closer. "Um." A series of emotions flickered over his face. "A baby is, uh, pretty amazing news, Makenna. But why do I feel like there's more?"

She hugged herself and nodded. "Because—"

"What does Caden have to say about this?" Patrick asked, his expression as serious as a heart attack. His narrowed eyes had her feeling like he'd already pieced this story together. It was the damn police officer in him.

"He doesn't know," she said, giving him a look that pleaded for his support.

"*What?*" Ian said.

"Why not?" Collin asked.

Everyone started talking at once, and her father hushed them all. "Tell us what's going on," he said, taking her hand.

"Um." She swallowed around the lump in her throat and fought back the emotion threatening to overwhelm her. "So, we broke up a few weeks ago. I'm not really sure what happened, to be honest. Caden had been really sick and stayed at his house. And then when I saw him after he was better, he just seemed off. He said we were moving too fast for him, and that was it. I'd just found out that I was pregnant and in the midst of everything, I didn't have a chance to tell him. And then I didn't want to tell him if that was the thing that would make him come back."

His expression full of concern, her father nodded. "How far along are you?"

"Almost twelve weeks," she said. "I'm seeing a doctor and everything looks good."

"Are you going to tell him?" Collin asked. All three of her brothers wore the same look on their faces—part concerned, part angry, but trying to rein the latter in.

"Yeah," she said. "I'm going to invite him to my next ultrasound, which isn't for over a month."

"So, you're keeping it?" Ian asked. Only the gentleness of his tone kept her from flipping out on him.

"Of course, I'm keeping it. This is my baby, too." The one bright spot of certainty in all of this was knowing without question or reservation that she *wanted* this baby. No matter what, he'd been conceived in love. And she already loved him. And if this was the only part of Caden she got to have, she was holding on tight with both hands. "So, that's…that's my news," she managed.

"Aw, you're going to be an amazing mother," her dad said, wrapping his arm around her shoulders. "And we'll be here for you every step of the way."

The unconditional support beckoned the tears she'd been holding back. Finally sharing this news with her family took such a weight off her shoulders. "Thanks," she whispered.

"And I'm sorry about Caden," her dad said as he pressed a kiss to her forehead. "I know this isn't easy."

She gave a quick nod, sniffling. "I'm sorry, too."

"Do you want me to talk to him?" Patrick asked, sitting forward next to her.

"About?" she asked, studying her brother's face.

He braced his elbows on his knees. "Just feels like something doesn't add up, Makenna. The guy I met on Thanksgiving was *way* into you. Then two weeks later, he's just up and done?" Patrick shook his head. "Something doesn't add up. And I'd kind of like to know what it is since Caden's presumably going to be in your life whether you're together or not."

Makenna was torn, especially since his instincts were on the money. There was more to it. And it had to do with Caden's history. In saying she deserved more than him, he'd all but laid that out. But his pain felt too private to share with them, even if it would help explain hers. "Let me think about it," she said, scrubbing at her cheeks. "But I appreciate it."

"Okay," Patrick said, clearly unhappy not to get the go-ahead. "Just say the word."

"Dad's right," Ian said. "You're gonna be great, Makenna."

"Yeah," Collin said. "And we're gonna be the most awesome uncles ever."

That set off a round of jokes and plans for the baby that had Makenna crying again, this time with happy tears. "Thank you," she said, her cheeks hurting from smiling. "Thank you for being here for me."

"That's what family's for," her dad said. "No matter what."

"No matter what," Patrick said, nodding.

"Absolutely," Ian said.

"No matter what, Sis," Collin said. "Except for changing poopy diapers. That's all Patrick."

Of course, her brothers couldn't pass up a good opportunity to make jokes about poop, which had them all laughing again. The tension bled out of Makenna's shoulders as she shook her head at them and laughed along. She was going to be okay, because she had these four amazing men standing at her side.

But who did Caden have?

CHAPTER NINETEEN

The new year hadn't made Caden a new man, but at least he was eating more and showering regularly and basically fucking functioning. Thanks to Joe. And twice-a-week sessions the past three weeks with Dr. Ward. And the wonders of modern pharmaceuticals.

Most of the time, it felt like he was making a slow climb up a steep mountain carrying a big-ass rock on his back, but at least he was climbing. That was a victory in and of itself. And he was working on giving himself some credit. Baby steps, man, that's what he was all about these days.

Sitting on the bed in Joe's guest room, Caden dragged the cardboard box full of unopened mail in front of him. Joe had brought it over from Caden's house after his shift the evening before. Now that Caden was rocking out all this basic functioning, it was time for him to try to take care of a few other key parts of his life. Like paying his mortgage. And keeping the damn electricity current so his place would have heat. Last thing he needed was to come home from this little sojourn at Chez Flaherty to find his pipes burst and his basement flooded.

He sorted through the box. Bill, bill, bill. Junk, junk, junk. Magazine, magazine. An invitation to the wedding of one of the guys at the station. More bills, some of them stamped *Second Notice*. Tons of fucking junk. A Christmas card.

He did a double take at the return address.

A Christmas card from Makenna.

He stared at it for a long moment. He'd walked out on her…and she'd sent him a Christmas card?

His gut clenched. He flipped the envelope over. Stared at the sealed flap. And finally ripped through it.

The card actually made him smile—and he couldn't remember when he'd last done that. It had a picture of a miserable blond-haired boy wearing a pink bunny costume and read, *He looks like a deranged Easter bunny!*

From *The Christmas Story* movie. A freaking classic.

Leave it to Makenna.

As fast as he'd managed that smile, it slid back off his face. They could've watched that together, sharing stupid humor movies like they always had. More than that, they could've celebrated Christmas together. Their first. If Caden hadn't fallen the fuck apart.

How much more of his present and his future was he going to let his past destroy?

Fuck.

He heaved a deep breath. *Eyes on the prize, Grayson.* Getting better. Getting whole. Rebuilding his life. And making right all the things he'd done wrong.

Hesitating just one more moment, he opened the card. There was no printed text on the inside, just Makenna's looping handwriting.

Dear Caden,

I just wanted you to know that I'm thinking of you. And if you need me, I'm here for you. I can't say I understand what happened between us, only that I'm willing to listen. I don't deserve more than you, because there is nothing more than you for me.

I still love...that elevator.

Merry Christmas,

Makenna

Caden read it over and over until he had the words memorized. He could still hear her voice saying *I love that elevator* that very first night they'd met. After hours of being trapped in the elevator and the most incredible sex of his life, she'd invited him to stay the night with her. When they'd settled into each other's arms, she'd blurted out, *I love...* And then she'd covered herself by adding *that elevator.* Caden had thought it was cute. It had given him hope that maybe she was feeling him with the same crazy intensity that he'd been feeling her. And in the days and weeks that followed, that had seemed to be true.

Until, somewhere along the way, he'd stopped trusting himself, the situation, his happiness, and maybe even her. He knocked his numb-ass skull back against the headboard. In that moment, he wouldn't have been surprised if a cartoon lightbulb suddenly appeared over his head. He'd stopped trusting her...not to abandon him. And so he'd done the leaving.

He'd made his own worst fears come true.

Brilliant fucking job.

Blowing out a long breath, he rubbed his fingers over what she'd written. *There is nothing more than you for me.* Could she really believe that? And could he get himself to a place where he did, too?

He picked up the envelope and found the postmark—she'd sent the card on December twentieth. Almost four weeks ago. He knew it was expecting too much to hope she might wait for him, to wait for him to be better. Not just for her, but for both of them. Especially when she had no way of knowing that he was trying to find his way back to himself, so he might earn a chance to come back to her.

He looked at what she'd written again. Once, twice, he swallowed around a lump that had lodged in his throat, and then he whispered, "Aw, Red. I still love that elevator, too."

The next week, Caden moved home and started back to work. He'd been off for almost six weeks and he was starting to go stir crazy sitting around Joe's house. It was time to get a life. His.

Truth be told, he was fucking nervous about walking back into the firehouse again. No doubt the rumors were flying about what had happened to him, especially given how bad a shape he'd been in those last few days on the job. And if the guys didn't have an idea of what might've been going on with him before, they'd probably get the gist just by looking at him—while he'd gained twelve pounds back so far, he was still down twenty from where he'd been at the beginning of December.

A shadow of his former self, maybe, but no longer a ghost.

Never again.

But his nerves would have to fucking suck it. Because he needed the work—not just for the money, but because he *needed* to help people. Right now, he was all about playing to his strengths, and doing his job had always been one. That much he could definitely give himself credit for.

He shouldn't have been worried.

To a man, they were nothing but happy to have him back. Even better, the day was a marathon of calls, one after the other, but it was smooth sailing all the way. Clocking out at the end of the shift made him feel ten feet tall. It had been just the confidence booster he needed.

And it gave him a little hope, too.

If he could get back on his feet at work, maybe, just maybe, that meant he could make things right in other parts of his life as well. Above all else, he wanted to make things right with Makenna.

Thinking of her made him ache, but less and less with unworthiness, guilt, and fear. No, this ache stemmed from the hollowness caused by their long separation, by her absence from his life. He missed her so bad that his chest often throbbed with it, like he'd left a part of himself in her hands. And he unquestionably had.

He just needed a little more time. A little more time to get himself right. A little more time to make peace with the past. A little more time to become the man that Makenna deserved and Caden wanted to be.

He just needed a little more time.

❦

A few nights later, Caden was sitting at his kitchen table writing out bills and suddenly found himself staring at the dragon tattoo on the back of his right hand and arm.

He saw it every day, of course. But for some reason, he hadn't actually *seen it* in a very long time. He hadn't remembered why it was there.

The tattoo had been a declaration and a promise. A declaration to himself that he'd conquered his fears, and a promise to his brother, Sean, that Caden would be strong, that Caden wouldn't live his life in fear when Sean couldn't live his at all.

"I forgot to be the dragon, Sean. But I won't forget again," he said out loud.

Which gave him an idea.

He placed a call, got lucky making an appointment, and booked it out of the house. Caden made it to Heroic Ink within twenty minutes.

"Glad you called, man," Heath said, extending his hand. "Been slow as fucking molasses in here all day."

Caden returned the handshake. "This is win-win then because I really wanted to get in tonight."

"Well, come on back and let's rock and roll," Heath said. "Flying solo?"

"Yeah," Caden said, the reference to Makenna not making him sad and regretful—for once, but making him even more confident in what he was about to do. Because clearly, he was in need of a new reminder, a new declaration, a new promise. And ink had always been part of his process for coping and healing.

"So tell me what you're thinking," Heath said, gesturing to the chair at his station.

"It's text. I want it on my left forearm, big as you can make it." As he sat, he handed Heath a sheet of paper he'd written on in the Jeep.

Heath nodded. "Want any embellishments? Flowers? Ribbon? Flourishes. Have any thoughts on font?"

"I'm open. You know what looks good, and I always like what you come up with. Just so the words are bold and the most prominent thing about the piece, I'll be happy," Caden said.

"Gimme ten to pull something together," Heath said, opening up his laptop. It didn't even take ten minutes. "What about something like this?"

Caden's gaze ran over the design on the screen. It was different from anything he'd imagined, so naturally it was perfect. "Do it. Just like that."

The first dig of the needles into his skin was like a balm to his soul. He'd *always* loved the feeling of getting a tattoo. He *liked* the pain because it reminded him he was alive. Enduring it always made him feel stronger. And each new piece always left him feeling like he'd donned a new plate in the suit of armor he'd spent a lifetime creating.

This one was no different.

What Heath had designed was intricate, and good-looking lettering took time, so Caden was there a long while. But he was totally fucking content. For once. Even though tattoos on the forearm hurt like a mofo.

About two and a half hours later, Heath said, "All done."

Caden hadn't been watching because he wanted to wait for the full effect when the tat was done. Now, he looked.

Solid black cursive words sat at an angle on his forearm in groups of twos, reading from his wrist to his inner elbow:

One Life / One Chance / No Regrets

Open-faced red roses flanked the top and bottom of the words and wrapped around his arm, while red and black flourishes curved out from some of the letters and around the flowers. The center of the bottom rose morphed into a clock with Roman numerals to remind him that time was always ticking—and wasting, if you didn't play things right. The way Heath had combined the elements looked phenomenal.

Caden might've survived that accident fourteen years before, but he'd never really understood why. He'd never really felt he had anything specific to live *for*. Meeting Makenna had changed all that, even if Caden had been too mired in the past to see it at the time. But now that he was working so hard to get himself healthy again, he saw it with a clarity that was startling.

Caden wanted a chance for a life with Makenna. And though he knew there was a chance she wouldn't take him back after what he'd done, he at least had to try.

"Fantastic work as always, Heath. Thank you," Caden said.

"Anytime. I hope it gives you what you need," Heath said, leaning in to bandage the piece.

"Me too," Caden said. "Me too." And though so much remained uncertain, Caden couldn't help but marvel at how far he'd come these past six weeks. Because, sitting there in that chair with his arm on fire, Caden's soul felt lighter than it had in longer than he could remember because he'd renewed his commitment to Sean.

And, more importantly, to himself.

CHAPTER TWENTY

Lying in bed on his day off, something Caden's therapist had said at his last session pinged around in his brain: *Find ways to close the door on the past.*

Caden had been thinking about it for days, wanting to find a way to do just that so he could start looking forward instead of always looking back. It was the last thing he needed to figure out before he'd feel ready to go after what he wanted.

Makenna James.

His gaze drifted to the stuffed bear on his nightstand, the one she'd given him to make him feel better. All these weeks, he'd kept it close—well, he hadn't slept with the damn thing because he was a twenty-eight-year-old man, after all—but he liked having something she'd touched close by.

And Makenna was what Caden most wanted. If she'd have him. And who the hell knew. Given the way he'd bailed on her— abandoned her, really, he might as well call a spade a fucking spade—he wouldn't blame her for slamming the door in his face.

Dr. Ward's advice had stemmed from discussing Caden's realization that he'd let the past control him so much that he'd made his own worst fears come true. The question was, what the hell did it mean to close the door on the past? How was Caden supposed to do that? All the people involved in the accident that he'd let define his life were gone. And he'd never been one who'd found any answers or solace in talking to gravestones.

The only thing that left was the scene of the accident itself.

Caden had never once gone back. Had never even thought about it. Truth be told, it scared him more than a little.

Which was probably why he should do it.

He gave it one last thought, and then he hauled his ass out of bed, showered, and got dressed. In his spare bedroom, he rooted through boxes of his father's things looking for the file from the insurance investigation into the accident. His father had died last August, and Caden hadn't kept many of the man's belongings—only the paperwork related to settling the estate, family photo albums that Caden hadn't even known his old man still had, and a few things from around the house that Caden had always associated with his mother. What he'd wanted of Sean's belongings Caden had claimed years before.

Caden was on his fifth box when he found what he was looking for. He pulled the thick folder from a stack and flipped it open. His gaze skimmed over things Caden didn't really want to re-read in detail—the specifics of his mother's and brother's injuries, first and foremost—until he found the location information for the accident that had occurred along Route 50 in Wicomico County, Maryland.

Bingo. Time for his biggest—and hopefully last—journey into the past.

The ninety-minute ride to the general area flew by, probably because Caden wasn't looking forward to confronting what he had to confront, but it took longer to find the actual stretch of highway where his family had crashed.

The investigation file listed a mile marker, which was the first piece of information he had to narrow his search, and there were also pictures of the accident itself. He'd seen them—and the whole file—before. When he was sixteen, he'd found the file and read it cover to cover, needing every gory detail like a junkie needed a fix. Caden had thought knowing would help, but it had just provided fodder for his subconscious to twist into nightmares and guilt and fear.

So he didn't spend a lot of time looking at the photographs now—except to take note of the fact that the ditch and field where the car had landed were immediately after a long line of trees, which was part of what had kept anyone that night from seeing the over-turned car for so many hours.

First, Caden saw the mile marker, and then he found the tree line. He pulled the Jeep onto the side of the road. Sitting in the driver's seat, Caden surveyed the scene, but beyond his knowledge of the photographs, not a thing there looked familiar. And why would it? The accident had occurred late at night and, by the time daylight broke, Caden had been out of his mind.

Taking a deep breath, Caden got out of the Jeep and walked around to the grass. The irrigation ditch was still there, creating a deep slope downward just a few feet off the edge of the road. He climbed into it. Stood there. Crouched down and placed his hand against the frozen earth where two people he'd loved had died.

Not a day goes by that I don't think of you, Mom and Sean. I'm sorry I lost you. I love you. And I'm trying so damn hard to make you proud.

Closing his eyes, he let his head hang on his shoulders.

A tractor trailer roared past, and the sound of it was familiar enough to send cold chills down Caden's back. But Caden wasn't trapped in that car. He *wasn't*. Not anymore.

He rose to his feet and looked around for one last minute. There weren't any ghosts there. There weren't any answers there. The past wasn't there.

The realization brought both relief and frustration. Relief that he'd come to this place and found it to be…just a place. Just an ordinary roadside sitting under the winter gray sky. Frustration because going there hadn't brought him any closer to figuring out how to close the door on the past.

What else could give him any sense of closure?

Back in the Jeep, he flipped through the investigation file. A name caught his attention. David Talbot. The paramedic who'd been the first person Caden was aware of on the scene of the accident. What Caden most remembered about the man was the kindness of his voice, the reassurances he kept offering, the way he explained everything that was happening even though Caden hadn't really been capable of following it. The man's words had helped ground Caden after a long night of not knowing what was real, and Caden had always been convinced that David Talbot was the only thing that had kept him from going insane. And staying there.

Holy shit, why hadn't Caden thought of Talbot before? Would the guy even be around? Maybe it was a long shot after fourteen years, but Caden's gut said there was something to this idea. It certainly couldn't hurt.

A quick search on his smart phone revealed that Talbot's firehouse in Pittsville was only a few minutes away. Caden made his way there not knowing what to expect, or whether he should expect anything at all.

The Pittsville Volunteer Fire Department was a two-building complex with the main firehouse having five bay doors, all of which stood open. Yellow and white fire and E.M.S. apparatus occupied each bay, and a line of pick-up trucks filled the lot off to one side. Caden pulled his Jeep in line with the trucks and hopped out.

His pulse kicked up a notch as he approached the firehouse, and his chest filled with an odd pressure borne of anticipation. He stepped into the bay housing a heavy rescue truck and headed in the direction of voices, but something caught his eye. A big number 7 on the side of the truck.

Prickles ran over Caden's scalp. Pittsville's fire department was Station 7? The same number as the station he worked in. The same station number he had tattooed on his biceps. What were the fucking chances?

"Can I help you?" came a voice from further inside.

Caden turned to see an older man with a beard and moustache standing by the end of the truck. "Yeah, sorry. My name is Caden Grayson. I'm E.M.S. over in Arlington County, Virginia," he said, extending a hand to the other man.

"Well, how 'bout that. Welcome. I'm Bob Wilson," the man said as they shook. "What brings you over our way?" he asked with a smile. One of the things Caden loved about working in fire and E.M.S.—the community you could find with others in the same line of work.

"Something personal, actually. An accident that happened fourteen years ago." Anticipation made Caden's gut feel like he was riding a roller coaster about to crest the highest hill. "Any chance a paramedic named David Talbot is still around?"

"Dave? Hell, yeah. We tried getting rid the guy but he just sticks to us like fleas on a dog." Bob smiled and winked.

"Shit, really?" Caden said, disbelief at this…*good luck* washing over him. "I knew it might be a long-shot."

"Nope. We're all pretty much long-timers here," Bob said, gesturing for Caden to follow. "Come on back. He's here. We had a call earlier, so you got lucky. Otherwise you woulda had to track him down at home."

As they made their way deeper into the big building, nervousness suddenly flooded through Caden's veins. The last time he and David Talbot had seen each other, Caden had been a wreck in every sense of the word. If anyone in Caden's life had seen him at his lowest, at his worst, at his most vulnerable, it was Talbot. Caden was so unprepared for the possibility of ever meeting this man—this man who represented such a positive force in Caden's life—that he wasn't sure what he was going to say.

Bob led them into the firehouse's dining room where eight men were sitting around the table talking and laughing, empty plates sitting in front of them. "Everyone," Bob said, "this is Caden Grayson. He's E.M.S. over in Arlington County, Virginia." A round of greetings rose up, and Caden gave a wave. "He came to see you, Dave."

Caden's gaze did a fast scan around the table, but he couldn't immediately identify Talbot. And then the man at the far end of the table turned to look at him, and Caden was suddenly sucked fourteen years into the past. When a man with a friendly face and a calming voice had put a traumatized fourteen-year-old kid at ease and saved his life.

"Me, huh?" Talbot said, rising and coming over to Caden. He extended a hand. "Dave Talbot. What can I do for you?"

Caden returned the shake, the oddest sense of déjà vu washing over him. "Well, Mr. Talbot, it's about what you've already done for me. Fourteen years ago, you were the first on the scene of a single-vehicle accident. And you saved my life."

What Caden needed to say was profoundly obvious, and he didn't even feel awkward about saying it in front of the other men who were all blatantly curious about what was going on.

"I know a long time has passed, but I need to say thank you. And I need to tell you that what you did for me that day made me want to help people, too. It's why I went E.M.S. I know we don't always get to know what happens to someone after we transport them to the hospital, so we don't get to know the impact we might've had. I wanted you to know that yours was huge. And I appreciate the hell out of it every day." Bone-deep satisfaction spread through Caden's bones at getting to pay respect to this man after all this time.

You could've heard a pin drop in that room.

Dave was visibly moved by Caden's words. The older man studied Caden's face then looked at the scar that jagged along the side of his head. "Well, I'll be damned," Dave said, his voice strained. "Overturned station wagon?" he said, almost as if thinking out loud.

"Yeah," Caden said, a lump lodging in his throat.

"I remember you," Dave said, clasping Caden's arm. "It's a real pleasure to see you, son." He shook his head and cleared his throat, emotion plain on his face. "This is a helluva thing right now. Damn."

"I remember that call," another of the men said, coming around the table to join them. "Some of them stick with you, especially when there are kids involved, and that was one for me." The man extended a hand. "Frank Roberts. I was real sorry for what you went through."

"Frank," Caden said, returning the shake. "Thank you. That means a lot."

"I was on that one, too, said a white-haired man sitting at the table. Damn impressed that you're in this line of work after that accident. A lot of people wouldn't be able to do that. Wallace Hart, by the way," he said, giving a little wave.

Caden nodded, just about as gobsmacked as he could be that these men were not only still here but actually remembered him, too. Remembered what had happened. His father had never been willing to discuss the accident. Hell, his father had barely talked to Caden beyond that which was strictly required for basic life logistics, so to find people after all this time who'd been there, who knew what'd happened, who'd known Caden then. Dave was right. That *was* a helluva thing.

"You have time to sit?" Dave asked. "I could grab you a cup of coffee. And we have pie."

A little overcome by their reaction to him, Caden nodded. "Does anyone say no to pie?"

"Not if they're in their right fucking mind," Frank said to a round of laughter.

Some of the men cleared out, leaving Caden, Dave, Frank, and Wallace at the table. The other three men all had a good twenty or more years on Caden, which maybe explained why they talked to and looked at him in almost a fatherly way. They asked about the aftermath of the accident, about what he'd done after school, about his training and station, and about his personal life—whether he had a family of his own.

"Not yet," Caden said, finishing the last bite of his apple pie. "Truth be told, I had someone, but I messed it up. I've struggled with PTSD and anxiety ever since the accident, and I let it get the best of me. I've been working on how to make it right. How to make *myself* right. I guess that's what led me here." It felt right to be honest with them. And, frankly, he was in the middle of a more meaningful conversation about his life than any he'd ever had with his own old man.

Sitting next to him, Dave nailed Caden with a stare. "Let me tell you something, Caden." He paused for a long moment. "We talked about you around here. Those of us on that call, we were all affected by what we encountered out there that morning, and we talked about it more than once. I'll tell you straight, every single one of us was surprised as hell that you survived that accident. Your father, too, though the rear section of the car was in the worst shape. I can still picture how flattened it was. Like it had gone through a compactor." The other men nodded. "Whatever difficulties you've faced, I imagine you came by them honestly after that. But you need to know that you surviving, that was a miracle to my mind."

"Yeah," Frank said. "You were damn lucky." Wallace nodded.

Lucky.

For so long, Caden hadn't believed such a thing existed, not for him. And here these men all agreed that's what he'd been. Had he been looking at it wrong all these years?

Emotion clogged Caden's throat and momentarily stole his ability to speak. He nodded. "I appreciate that because...because sometimes I've had to ask myself why I survived when my mother and brother didn't." He shook his head.

"It's the wrong question," Dave said. "A better one is, what happened *because* you survived? And I'll tell you. Because you survived, you went on to become a paramedic. And what you did today for me, by coming in here and telling me what my help meant to you? There are people out there who feel the same way about you. You may never meet them—hell, you probably won't, that's the nature of the thing—but they're out there for you just like you were for me. And I want to thank you for that, for what you said. Because this job makes you confront a lot of hard things and it takes you away from your family at all hours and it puts you in harm's way, so it's good to know that what I do—what we all do," he said, gesturing at all of them seated there, "matters."

"Amen to that," Wallace said, raising his coffee cup and taking a swig.

As Dave's words sank in, Caden felt a little like he'd walked cartoon-like into a pole he hadn't seen coming. The idea that Caden might matter to someone as much as Dave did to Caden, the idea that what Caden did for his patients might impact them the same way Dave's care had impacted Caden all those years ago…it was fucking *revelatory*.

His scalp prickled and his heart raced. All these years that Caden had wasted feeling worthless and guilty, wondering what the point of his surviving had been, he'd always thought of his work as paying a debt he owed. And there was truth in that. But there was truth in what Dave said, too.

What Caden did mattered to a lot of people.

Which meant that *he* mattered, whether he felt it or not.

Damn. *Damn.*

That idea parked itself on Caden's chest like a thirty-ton ladder truck. That shit wasn't going *anywhere*.

It was like sunlight breaking through heavy black clouds, the golden rays streaming in and touching everything in their paths. Illuminating things that had been dark for so long. Shedding light on things long forgotten. It was a lightness of being that Caden couldn't ever remember feeling before. Soul-healing relief rushed in behind the light, along with the unimaginable—forgiveness.

And not just for himself.

Had Caden's father ever had anyone to talk to about the accident? Because if Caden felt guilt just for surviving, what must his father have felt for being the one behind the wheel?

The question was another eye-opener, one that had his heart letting go of some of the anger Caden had carried for over half of his life. And more of that light streamed in.

Before long, he was exchanging contact information with Dave and the others and saying his good-byes. And Caden felt like he'd finally figured out Dr. Ward's advice. Because an hour with the men who'd saved his life had done more to give him closure on the accident than anything else in the past fourteen years.

"Hey, Caden," Dave called as Caden was heading out of the bay.

Caden turned. "Yeah?"

Dave gave him a serious look. "If I've learned anything, it's that little matters more than family and love. Do whatever you have to do to win back that girl."

"I'm going to do everything I can," Caden said.

And after today, he finally felt like he might be ready.

CHAPTER TWENTY-ONE

Makenna left her four-month check-up and knew the time had come—she had to tell Caden about the baby. The ultrasound appointment was in two weeks, and there was no reason to keep putting the conversation off, except that she was nervous as hell about doing it.

Driving through the early evening darkness, Makenna made her way to Caden's house. This conversation couldn't happen by phone or text or email. She had to do it face to face—not just because it was the right way to go about it, but because she needed to see Caden. To see how he was. To see how he reacted to the news. She just needed to see *him*.

Because Caden Grayson was an ache inside her that wouldn't go away.

She pulled into his cul-de-sac to find his house dark and his parking place empty. Echoing the trip she'd made over a month ago, she drove to the little firehouse on the other side of Fairlington—but this time she found his Jeep.

He'd gone back to work.

Makenna's chest swelled with emotion. If he'd gone back, that must mean he was okay, and that made her happy. But the fact that he'd gone back to work—but not come back to her—really must mean that whatever sliver of hope she'd been holding out for them was completely pointless.

If he was going to come back, he'd have done it.

At least, now she knew.

Anyway, that's not what telling him about the baby was about. More than that, she didn't want Caden back if the baby was the only reason he wanted to be in her life. So. Fine.

As she parked her car along the curb, the clock on the dash said that it was nearly 5:30. His shift probably ended at seven tonight or seven tomorrow morning, depending on the schedule—the firehouse had an overlapping shift system to ensure they were always staffed and could give the guys adequate days off after working twenty-four hours at a time. Which meant she could either go in there and talk to him. Or she could wait.

After waiting two months, she would've thought the idea of a few more hours would've been nothing. But knowing Caden was just across the street in that building—so close—after all this time apart nearly had Makenna crawling out of her skin.

She'd given him time and space. Just like he'd asked. Now she was done with that. This baby was coming whether either of them was ready or not.

Without letting herself overthink it any further, Makenna shut off the car and got out. Flurries whirled around her, and she ducked her head against the freezing wind and zipped her thick coat up to her neck.

On a nice day, the guys often had the doors to the bays open, their trucks on display. But those doors were closed up tight against this weather, so Makenna headed to the office door on the side. Belly going for a loop-the-loop, she let herself into the reception area, setting off a buzzer. No one stood behind the counter.

After a few seconds, a young guy she didn't know came in from the back. "Can I help you?"

"Hi," she said. "Is Caden Grayson here?"

"Grayson? Yeah." He gave her an appraising look that rushed heat into her cheeks. "I'll get him."

The guy disappeared into the hallway beyond. "Grayson!" he yelled, making Makenna's cheeks burn a little hotter. "Visitor."

Makenna stuffed her hands in her pockets and blew out a shaky breath.

An exchange of words down the hall caught her ear—because she heard Caden's voice. Hearing it was a relief and a heartache. She braced in anticipation of seeing him walk through the door.

And then he did.

Be strong, Makenna.

"Hi," she said, drinking him in with her eyes. He looked…so fucking good. Gorgeous, as always, with that strong jaw and that masculine face and those broad shoulders. He was a little thinner, but the dark circles were nearly gone from beneath his eyes and everything about him seemed…lighter somehow. Like he stood taller, moved easier.

"Makenna, what are you doing here? Are you okay?" he asked, coming around the counter to her. He stopped an arm's length away.

"I'm sorry to bother you at work, but I—"

"No, I'm sorry." He rubbed his hand over the scar on his head. "I didn't mean it that way. Just surprised, is all."

"I know. I was hoping we could talk for a minute. It shouldn't take long," she said. Well, actually, it was going to take the next eighteen years, at least. But what needed to happen just then shouldn't take long.

"Uh, yeah. Yeah, of course," he said. "Come inside with me?"

Her heart squeezed as a little voice inside her said, *I'd follow you anywhere, Caden. Don't you know that?* But all she said was, "Sure."

She followed him around the counter, a ridiculous little thrill fluttering through her when their arms brushed as they walked down the white cinder-block hall.

For some reason, that sensation made her think of the first time she ever touched him. That night they were trapped in the elevator. After maybe two hours, they'd both gotten hungry and shared two snacks and a bottle of water that Makenna had in her bag. Because they couldn't see one another to hand off the water, they'd slid it back and forth across the floor until they encountered the other person's hand. By then, she'd already learned just how much they had in common and become intrigued by Caden, and those little touches from a man she'd talked to but never seen had been thrilling.

Walking beside Caden after so long apart, that night seemed like it'd happened a million years before.

Laughter and trash talk spilled out of a room off to the left. Having been to the station before, Makenna knew it was the kitchen and dining room. A quick peek in as they passed it revealed that the table was full, and all the guys had plates of food in front of them. She caught Bear's eye as she and Caden walked by.

"I'm sorry I interrupted your dinner," she said, peering up at Caden.

"Don't be," he said in a quiet voice.

At the end of the hall, they turned to the right. "Let's, uh, let's go in here," he said, pushing a door open for her. He flicked on the light, revealing two rows of bunk beds along the walls, all neatly made.

The door shut, closing them in together.

Makenna's heart tripped into a sprint.

Caden's gaze raked over her and finally settled on her face, his eyes filled with an intensity she didn't understand. "You look really great, Makenna."

"Uh, thanks," she said, the compliment catching her off guard. "You look good, too. Better." Better than before, she thought, but she didn't want to get caught up in talking about the past when what she needed to discuss with him was the future. "So—"

"Did you have a good Christmas?" he asked, stepping a little closer.

She tilted her head, trying to read him. "Um. Sure. I went home to Philly. It was…it was nice."

On top of the awkwardness, an odd tension filled the space between them, like they were magnets that didn't know whether they were supposed to attract or repel.

Because the attraction was definitely there—at least for her. Her body was hyperaware of his. How much taller than her he was. How close he stood. How broad his chest was. How his hands fisted and his jaw ticked.

He reached out and fingered the end of her hair, then seemed to think better of it and pulled his hand away. "Your hair's gotten longer."

The fleeting touch had Makenna's heart pounding in her chest. Desire and yearning roared through her, and she didn't know whether to be annoyed at herself for responding that way or climb him. Or both.

"Yeah," she managed. "I just haven't gotten around to it." She shrugged, because why they were talking about her hair, she wasn't sure. "Look, Caden," she said, wanting to take control of things. "I need to—"

Dooodo, dooodo, dooodo

The tones of the station alerting system sounded loudly in the small space and blue and red lights on the ceiling started flashing—the color combination communicated that they had a fire and medical call. Caden had taught her that the first time she'd visited there. The dispatcher's voice spilled from a speaker in the ceiling with the details of the call.

"Shit," Caden said, his face going serious but his eyes filled with something that looked a lot like disappointment. "I'm really sorry, but I gotta go."

Makenna's stomach fell. "I know," she said. "Duty calls."

"I'd rather stay and talk to you," he said, stepping closer, so close that she could've leaned forward and his chest would've easily cushioned her weight. "I don't know how long I'll be. This day has been a bear, and the freezing rain we're supposed to get tonight probably means more of the same," he rushed out.

She caught the scent of his clean, crisp aftershave. "Will you promise to call me? When you have time to talk. As soon as you can?" Makenna nailed him with a stare.

Heated brown eyes blazed down at her—or maybe that was her projecting what she felt and what she wished. "I'm on tomorrow, too, but I can promise that."

"I mean it, Caden," she said.

And then he stole her breath. He cupped the back of her head in his hand and pressed a kiss to her forehead, then one to her cheek. He nuzzled the side of her face. "I promise," he said.

Oh God. His heat, his touch, this confusing moment of bliss. It ended in an instant.

"I'm sorry. You know your way out, yeah?" he said, already opening the door.

Stunned, all Makenna could do was nod. "Be careful," she called.

But he was already gone.

And Makenna had no idea how to interpret what'd just happened.

Fuck. Fuckfuckfuck.

That was the general tenor of Caden's thoughts as he and his partner pulled out of the bay in response to the call. He couldn't believe…so much. That Makenna had come to see him. That he'd had her right there in front of him. And that they'd been interrupted before he could say even one of the things that needed to be said.

And before she could tell him why she'd come. Curiosity curled through his gut. Why *had* she come to see him? After all this time? He was dying to know, but wasn't sure what the next thirty-six hours of his double shift might entail for him given the shit show bad weather usually created. And he didn't want to leave anything up to chance. Glad he wasn't driving for this one, he pulled out his phone and shot off a text.

It was damn good to see you, Red. Do you maybe want to get together Friday night to talk? I'm serious about keeping my promise.

Not just the one he'd made to call her, but the one he'd made to himself to live with no regrets.

He hit *Send* and nearly held his breath.

Makenna responded in less than a minute. *I have an on-site meeting in Loudoun County on Friday and won't get home until late. Saturday morning? It was good to see you, too.*

That last line made him smile, even though having to wait an extra night was going to kill him. The only reason he hadn't driven right from the Pittsville FD to Makenna's apartment the day before was because he'd wanted to touch base with his therapist first. Just to make sure he'd thought all this through the right way. Because when Caden went to Makenna, he wanted it to be for keeps. If by some miracle she was willing to give him a second chance, he didn't want to do anything to fuck it up. Ever again.

He texted back. *Saturday morning works. Your place, or?*

My place. Be careful, Makenna replied.

You, too, Red. Caden's fingers itched to type more. But he'd wait. Because now he knew exactly when he'd have his shot to get the life he most wanted.

And this time, nothing was going to stand in his way.

CHAPTER TWENTY-TWO

The traffic on 66 was heavy but moving as Makenna made her way home on Friday night from the off-site meeting she'd had out west of D.C., which was surprising given the snow and freezing rain they'd had on and off all day. Being from Pennsylvania, Makenna wasn't uncomfortable driving in the snow, whereas people in D.C. tended to either crawl along or drive like maniacs who didn't think frozen surfaces and black ice could possibly affect them. But so far, so good.

Makenna's stomach did a little flip. Only one more sleep until she'd see Caden tomorrow and finally get to tell him her news. *Their* news.

As if she wasn't nervous enough, seeing him on Wednesday night had confused the hell out of her. His compliments, his touches, his *kisses*. The text he'd sent saying how good it was to see her. What did all of that mean?

And was she being a complete and hopeless idiot for wanting it to mean that he still had feelings for her? Because she would've given almost anything for that to be true. Even after everything.

It didn't seem to matter what she told her heart, because it wouldn't stop wanting the sweet, sexy, damaged man she'd met in the darkness.

A song came on and she hummed along until she couldn't hold back from singing the catchy tune on the chorus. Paying close attention to the road, her gaze shifted from the cars in front of her to her rear view mirror as she sang.

A tingling sensation in her belly. Again.

Makenna didn't think anything about it.

Until it happened again. Harder. Like... *Oh, my God!* Like something moved inside her.

Could that have been the baby? She was suddenly sure it was.

"Was that you peanut?" she asked out loud, a smile breaking out on her face like she hadn't felt in weeks. She nearly held her breath for the sensation to happen again, because the first fluttery feeling of her baby moving inside of her was one of the most amazing things she'd ever felt. "Do that again, you little bugger."

The rest of the song played out, and the baby didn't move again, but that didn't keep Makenna from grinning until her cheeks hurt.

Slam!

Something hit the rear quarter-panel of her car on the driver's side, and Makenna barely had time to make out the shape of a dark SUV spinning out of control before she was struggling to control her own car. The impact of the other vehicle sent her Prius into a slow sliding circle. She turned her steering wheel in the other direction, trying as hard as she could to keep from losing control.

"No, no, no, no, no."

Her efforts were keeping the car from spinning out, but the hit had pushed her onto the snow-covered side of the road untreated by the plows and salt trucks. Her tires lost traction, and the car wouldn't respond to her handling or to the brakes she reluctantly engaged as other cars' brakes lights came on ahead of her.

"Oh God, oh God, oh God," she said out loud, because she wasn't going to be able to stop. And flashing headlights behind her revealed she wasn't the only one out of control.

Airbags exploded in front of her with a cracking *pop*, and then her car became a pinball.

She hit a car ahead of her and slammed into the airbag. There was no time to think or feel or react. *Pop.* The side airbags deployed, and she was hit again. Again. Again. The car jolted this way and that. Screeching tires and blaring horns and other crashes sounded out all around her until Makenna couldn't tell from which direction they came. Another hit, the hardest yet. Suddenly the car was on its side and rolling.

And all Makenna could do was scream.

Caden's cell phone rang a little after seven, and he picked it up to see the firehouse's number on his screen. "Grayson here."

"Caden, it's Joe. I know you just pulled a double but there's a multi-vehicle MVA on 66 I expect us to get called in for any minute now. I sent Olson home an hour ago with the flu so we're short and I know you're close," his captain said.

Caden was already shoving on his boots. "I'll be there in five."

By the time Caden was parking his Jeep, the doors on the firehouse bays were rolling up. Both emergency vehicles had their lights flashing as men suited up and climbed in. Caden hightailed it through the falling snow to the rig and grabbed his gear. "Let's rock and roll," he said as he jumped into the passenger seat of the paramedic unit.

From the engine truck, Joe gave him a salute.

"Catch me up," Caden said to Brian Larksen, driving the rig beside him. They'd run many an incident together over the years.

"Multiple vehicles. Possibly as many as ten. Two overturned. One, Two, and Three are on the scene or en route," Larksen said, referring to the county's other fire stations. "Four and Ten were called out with us."

"Christ, what a mess." Caden said. "Well, one patient at a time."

"Just like we do," Larksen said, hauling ass onto Interstate 395 behind the engine truck.

Even with Friday night traffic and the snow, they made it to the scene in just under fifteen minutes. Not bad for being outside their usual area of operation.

And, Jesus, the scene was a fucking disaster.

Even from a distance, Caden could see the responders struggling to access vehicles smashed one against the next. A delivery truck was on its side half in the grass, where the road sloped down toward the exit ramp for Westmoreland Street.

They caught up with their guys at the engine, awaiting orders from the chief running the incident. Orders came quickly, and Caden and Larksen were tasked with attending the driver of the delivery truck. They got their gear and booked it to the truck. The crash had blown out the windshield, making access to the passenger cab easier than it otherwise would've been.

"Sir, my name's Caden Grayson. I'm with Arlington E.M.S. and I'm going to help you," Caden said, leaning in through the jagged edges of the busted window. The male driver was laying against the passenger door, which was road-side down, likely revealing he hadn't been wearing his seat belt. The man looked up, and the side of his face was like hamburger. "Just lay real still for me. We're gonna get you out of there. What's your name?"

"Jared," the man rasped.

"Getting him out of there is going to be a bear," Larksen said quietly, handing Caden a flashlight. Caden nodded, his brain already working through the logistics on this one. They might need an assist.

Caden knocked out the rest of the glass along one edge so he could lean over without cutting himself.

"Jared," Caden said, leaning in further. "I'm going to take your vitals. Can you tell me what hurts?"

"My face and my arm," the man said. "I got dragged against the road here."

"Do you think anything's broken?" Caden asked, getting the man's pulse and heart rate, and checking the dilation of his eyes.

"No. I don't think so," Jared said.

"Okay, buddy, just hang in there. I'll be right back," Caden said, unfolding himself from around the window. He was updating Larksen and gathering supplies when Jared's voice sounded from behind him.

The man was trying to climb out.

"Whoa, whoa," Caden said, turning to support the man's shoulders as he leaned out the window, blood streaming down his face and onto Caden's jacket.

Larksen was right there, and together they lifted him out and laid him down on the road.

"Grayson!" a voice called.

Caden looked around until he saw Bear jogging toward him, but he ignored the other man because they had to get these wounds treated, particularly the one on Jared's face. White bone glinted through the gore, and now Jared was struggling to maintain consciousness.

"Grayson," Bear said, running up beside him.

"What?" Caden said, laser-focused on his patient.

"I need you to come with me," Bear said.

He held out his bloody gloves. "Little busy here."

"Shit, Caden. I need you to come with me *now*." Something about Bear's tone slid ice into Caden's veins.

"I got this," Larksen said. "Deal with whatever it is and come back."

Caden rose, rolling off his gloves and dropping them to the ground. "What's the problem?"

Bear took him by the arm and led him away from the truck and further onto the grass that divided the highway from the exit ramp that curved off down a little hill. "She's conscious, but she's trapped, and she's—"

"What the hell are you talking about, Bear?" Caden asked, agitated at having been pulled away.

"Makenna," Bear said, pointing down the slope, where a little car sat upside down and propped at an angle against the hillside.

The world sucked in on Caden until he couldn't see anything else. He took off like a shot, sprinting his way down the slippery embankment, his heart in his throat, his gut a sick knot, his brain paralyzed with fear.

No, no, no, not Makenna!

Firefighters were working on opening the badly mangled driver's door so they could extricate, so Caden slid around to the passenger side where a team of paramedics was working.

"Makenna!" he called. "Makenna?"

"Caden?" she cried, her voice warped and wobbly.

A gray-haired EMT from Station Four named Max Bryson peered awkwardly out of the door. "Caden, she's been asking for you." Caden swallowed hard as the man climbed out of the crumpled, upside-down front passenger seat. "She's stable for now. I can't tell about the baby though, I'm sorry. They'll have her out in just a few. Car's stable if you want to get in with her."

"Baby?" he asked, his brain scrambling to catch up with the man's words.

"Shit, you didn't know?" Bryson asked.

Makenna's pregnant? Caden's head was spinning.

But he wasn't what mattered.

Caden crouched down to the narrow opening of the crushed passenger seat immediately. "Makenna?" Jesus, it was tight. And that was as much thought as he gave that before crawling in beside her because fuck his claustrophobia. Nothing was keeping him away from her.

He couldn't quite get his whole body into the space, but he was close enough to see that she was hanging upside down by her seat belt, her body curled by the way the loss of roof height forced her to bend.

Christ, she was bleeding and cut up and shaking. White powder from the airbag deployments dusted her hair, face, and clothing.

Every one of her injuries lashed at his soul. "Makenna, talk to me."

"Oh, God, it r-really is y-you. Caden, I'm-I'm s-scared," she said, looking up at him, her face wet with tears and blood from a wound that had been bandaged on the side of her forehead.

He reached for her hand, but found it wrapped in gauze and splints. "It's me. I'm here."

"The baby," she whispered, her tears coming harder. "I don't w-want to lose your baby."

The words reached into his chest and squeezed so hard he could barely breathe. He had so many questions, but now wasn't the time. "Everything's gonna be okay," he said, willing it with everything inside him. Life owed him this, goddammit. This one thing. Her and his child coming out of this okay. The fucking bullshit in his head had robbed him of so much already. Not this. Not this, too. He crawled closer so that he could rub her hair. "You're pregnant, Red?" The wonder of those words raced through him.

"I'm s-sorry," she cried. "I should've t-told you sooner, but I...I..." Her face crumpled.

"No, no," he said, stroking her hair. "Don't worry. I won't let anything happen to you or the baby, okay? I promise." Jesus, she was pregnant. *Pregnant*. With his baby. He'd be fucking ecstatic about that if he knew they were both okay.

With a loud crunch, the driver's side door abruptly wrenched open. Makenna flinched on a moan.

"Hey, Red, look at me. They're going to get you out of here. Just hold on for another minute," Caden said, looking into her beautiful eyes. It killed him to see so much pain and fear there. "Take a nice deep breath for me." She did. "Another," Caden said, breathing with her, calming her down.

"Okay, Makenna," Bryson said, leaning in the doorway. "We're gonna cut your seatbelt free and ease you out of there. Caden? You think you can support her legs from in there so I can get her out by the head and shoulders?"

"Yes," Caden said without hesitation. Although it was going to force him to squeeze all of himself into the tight space so he'd have leverage to hold her. They didn't want her to fall to the roof of the car when they cut her free. He got into position, his shoulder bracing her thighs. His head was crammed against the jagged roof.

Which was the first moment it occurred to him that he and Makenna were stuck together in a crashed upside-down car. *Déjà fucking vu.*

The moment Bryson cut the belt, Caden was all that was holding her. Makenna gasped as her weight shifted. "I've got you, Red. I've got you."

Judging by the way her legs turned, Bryson was slowly moving her upper body toward the opening. She groaned and her hands flew to her belly. "Please, please, please, please," she whispered over and over again.

And Caden was right there with her. *Please let them both be okay.*

As Bryson started to move her out of the car, Caden slowly lowered her legs into his arms, and then another guy outside grasped her legs until she was free.

Getting himself back out of the car took longer than he had patience for, but he essentially had to soldier crawl under what was left of the caved-in passenger door opening. And then he scrambled around to the far side and went to his knees by Makenna's head.

As he leaned over her, words spilled out of his mouth in a desperate rush. He couldn't let another second pass without her knowing. "I love you, Makenna. I've loved you from the very beginning, since you laughed in that elevator and eased my fears, since you shared your first-time story with me and made me laugh, since you accepted me even when I couldn't accept myself. I'm so fucking sorry," he said.

"Caden?" she said, her voice slurring. Her eyelids fluttered and sagged.

"Yeah, Red, it's me," he said.

Her head lolled to the side.

"Loss of consciousness," one of the medics said. "Let's get her moving."

Caden rose as the men lifted the stretcher. "I'm going with you," he said to Bryson, daring the man with his gaze to challenge him. He didn't. Jogging along with the stretcher, they made for Station Four's paramedic unit. Caden glanced around for his team, and saw Bear in the distance. The guy looked his way and gave him a wave and a nod. It was all the okay he needed, and if there was hell to pay for leaving, Caden was more than willing to pay it.

Because everything he loved lay broken and bleeding at his side. Here he'd thought he had time…time to get himself right so he could be the man Makenna deserved. Now, all he could do was hope he wasn't too late.

CHAPTER TWENTY-THREE

Caden was climbing the walls. Once they'd reached the emergency department, the staff had made him wait while Makenna was triaged and treated. But there was one thing he could do to fill the crawling time. Her family needed to know what'd happened.

At Thanksgiving, Caden and Patrick had exchanged information. He found her brother's number and waited as it rang.

"Patrick James here," he answered.

"Patrick, it's Caden Grayson, Makenna's—"

"I know who you are, Caden." The ice in the other man's tone made it crystal clear that Patrick knew what'd gone down between him and Makenna. "To what do I owe the call?"

"Makenna was in an accident. She's stable but in the hospital. Came in by ambulance fifteen minutes ago," Caden said, hating to be the bearer of this news when he knew how close Patrick and Makenna were.

"Fuck," Patrick said. "What happened? Is she injured? How's the baby?"

Patrick knowing about the baby made Caden feel grateful that Makenna hadn't been dealing with that all on her own. Caden should've been there, but at least she'd had her family. "She was semi-conscious and banged up when she came in but her injuries weren't serious, although they haven't determined the baby's condition yet. Ten-car pile-up on Interstate 66. Makenna's Prius got flipped over a guard rail and overturned." Caden scrubbed his hand over his scar as he paced in the busy waiting room.

"I'm going to get the family together and we'll get down there as fast as we can. Where are you?" Patrick asked. Caden gave him the hospital information, and then Patrick said, "Thanks for calling me, Caden. I appreciate it. But I need you to be prepared to answer some questions for me when we get Makenna squared away. You hearing me?"

"A hundred percent. I'll be happy to tell you anything you want to know," Caden said. "I love her, Patrick. I fucked up, but I love her."

A long pause, and then, "We'll see you soon." Patrick hung up.

Caden couldn't spare any worry for the James men's reactions to him, not when every cell in his body agonized over what was going on with Makenna. Besides, any anger they bore toward him he'd earned with his mistakes. So he understood that he'd have to work to earn back their trust. He'd be fucking happy to grovel to anyone who wanted that from him if it would make Makenna and their baby okay.

Their baby. Every time he thought about Makenna's pregnancy, the wonder of it smacked him upside the head anew. Sheer awe lit up his chest. There was fear inside him, too, he wasn't going to deny that. Fear for this little, vulnerable life, maybe struggling to survive. Fear that he would be responsible for protecting and guiding that life. Fear of the million unknowns that could rain down on you at absolutely any moment.

As tonight proved.

But the wonder, the awe, the light—the love—all of it was so much bigger than the fear. So much more powerful. It was the fiery brightness of the sun against the cool glow of the moon.

No matter what happened, Caden had a family. Right this very minute. For the first time in over fourteen years.

And he wanted that family more than he'd ever wanted anything in his life.

"Makenna James family?" a blond-haired woman wearing scrubs called from the doors to the emergency department.

Caden rushed over. "I'm her boyfriend," he said. The word was so fucking inadequate compared to what she was to him—his everything.

The doctor guided him inside past patients waiting in cubicles, on gurneys, and in chairs. "I'm Dr. Ellison. Makenna's awake and stable. She's cramping a little and the baby's heartrate is elevated, but otherwise the baby seems to be fine. The next twelve to twenty-four hours will give us more information." They turned a corner into a hallway with curtained rooms. "She needs an X-ray on her hand and a CT scan for the head injury. We've got those orders in, but radiology's backed up so we're in a holding pattern. Hopefully it won't be too long." The doctor stopped at the edge of a curtain. "Any questions?"

Only about a million, but none that he needed the doctor to answer. "No, thanks."

With a nod, Dr. Ellison drew back the striped curtain and stepped into the small room. And there was his Makenna, bandaged and bruised with IVs protruding from her hand, but alive and awake. And without question the most beautiful thing Caden Grayson had ever seen in his life.

Makenna felt like she was moving slower than everything around her, or maybe that was just the pain meds they'd given her. Sounds came as if from a distance. The walls seemed a little wavy. Her limbs were like lead.

The curtain to her room suddenly opened and the doctor walked in…*with Caden!*

"Makenna," Dr. Ellison said, "I have Caden here for you. I've updated him on your condition. We're just waiting on radiology, okay?" The woman patted Makenna's arm.

"Okay," Makenna said in a weak voice, her gaze glued to Caden. He wore his uniform, his coat dirty with mud and blood here and there. "Thank you."

"Press the call button if either of you need anything," Dr. Ellison said, and then she was gone.

Caden shrugged out of his coat and dropped it on a chair, and then it was like he was stuck there at the edge of the room. She ached for him to come to her, but all she could manage was his name before she started crying. "Caden…"

He was to her in an instant, his body folding over her, his forehead settling against hers. "I'm sorry, Makenna. I'm so fucking sorry," he said.

Makenna shook her head as her mind struggled to process his words. "It wasn't your fault," she said. "I was just glad you were there. I was praying for it, actually, so hard. When you showed up, I wasn't sure whether to believe you were real."

Caden reached behind him and dragged a chair as close to her bedside as he could. He sat heavily and cradled her hand against his big chest. "I'm not talking about the accident," he said, dark eyes blazing. "I'm talking about how I left you, how I shut you out, how I lost myself and didn't know how to own up to it with you." He swallowed thickly, his Adams apple bobbing in his throat. "I'm talking about making you go through finding out you were pregnant all by yourself, making you worry for even a second that you would have to raise a child by yourself." He shook his head, and she'd never seen his expression more earnest.

Relief flooded through her that he'd accepted the idea of the baby so readily, and that he seemed to want to be involved. Which meant that her little one wouldn't have to grow up with only one parent as Makenna had, after all.

"Do you remember what I said after they pulled you from the car?" he asked, his eyes on fire with an intensity that reached inside her chest and just...owned her.

But Makenna couldn't remember anything after the scare of her car door screeching open. They'd cut her loose from the seat belt, and then... It was all a blur. "No," she whispered. "What did you say?" Her heart tripped into a sprint because the moment felt weighted with a significance she didn't understand and didn't want to read too much into. She wouldn't be able to withstand the disappointment and heartache. Not after the scares this night had entailed.

"I said...I said that I love you, Makenna. I said—"

"Because of the baby," she threw out, fear getting the best of her. But she had to know.

"Yes, because of the baby—"

"Caden—"

"Makenna, I've been in love with you since the night we met. I'm as sure of that as I am that I let my family's accident dictate my life in ways I wasn't even aware of—until I totally crashed and burned. I love you so much if feels like a part of me is gone when we're not together. I love you because you're beautiful and kind and smart and funny. Because you accepted me when I didn't even accept myself. Because your heart is more filled with empathy and understanding than anyone I've ever met. I don't make any sense without you. Not anymore. Because you're in me, and I want you there. I want you there forever. You *and* the baby. Our baby."

"You...you love me?" she asked, trying the words out as emotion ballooned inside her chest. "Then why...*why?*" Awkwardly, she tried to scrub away the tears from her face, but the bandages on one hand and the IV in the back of the other made it nearly impossible.

Caden grasped a tissue from the box on the rolling tray, and then he leaned in and dried her tears for her. It was such a ridiculously tender gesture that Makenna sucked in a breath.

"Why did you walk away?" she asked again.

With a heavy sigh, Caden sat back down and took her hand again. He pressed a lingering kiss to her knuckles, the little caring gestures lending credence to his words. "The short answer is that I lost myself, I let myself spiral until I couldn't control it, and then I became clinically depressed."

"Oh, Caden," she said, the knowledge that he'd been hurting so badly cutting right through her.

He shook his head. "I'm better now, so don't worry. I've been working on getting myself back on track for months. And I *am* better, Red, I need you to know that. Better than I've ever been since the accident." Another kiss to her knuckles. "I let a lot of things chip away at my confidence until I'd convinced myself I didn't deserve you—"

"I don't love Cameron, Caden. I don't want him. And I want you to know I've asked him never to contact me again," she rushed out.

"I know you don't love him. I know you were honest and sincere in everything you said to me. Problem was, I couldn't hear what you were saying, or I couldn't let myself believe it. I don't know. And that's another thing I should apologize for," he said, lips pressing into a hard line. "That I let my lack of faith in myself affect the faith I had in you. And I fucking hate that I did that. Because you did nothing to warrant it. It was all my own bullshit. But that realization was why I was waiting to come back to you, to come back and ask for a second chance. I wanted to come back to you whole. I wanted to be healthy. I wanted to be confident I wouldn't make the same mistakes all over again. I couldn't do that to you."

"And are you all those things now?" she asked, hope and pride rising up inside her. Because there was something in the light in his eyes and the strength of his words that had already answered the question.

"Yes," he said, nodding, his gaze burning into hers. "For the first time, yes. I had been planning to see you this weekend, even before you stopped by the station Wednesday night." He gave a little shrug. "You showing up felt like a sign. That it was time. And that I was ready."

Makenna closed her eyes and inhaled a deep breath, all the stressful uncertainty she'd been carrying sloughing right off her shoulders. It was the most beautiful relief, even as exhaustion from the night stole over her body. Looking at him again, she gave a small smile. "I'm so proud of you, Caden."

"So," he said in a low voice. "Do you think…could you give me a second chance to be in your life? To love you? You and the baby?"

"Oh, Caden, I've just been waiting for you to say the words," she said, her throat going tight. "I want you in my life more than anything, and not a second has passed since we've been apart that I haven't loved you with everything that I am." She rubbed her knuckles along the prominent ridge of his cheekbone and wished her body was in a condition that would let her do what she really wanted—to climb into his lap, wrap herself around him, and never let go. "I'm going to love you forever. I'm not going anywhere, no matter what."

"Jesus, Makenna, I was so damn scared you'd be done with me for good," he said, stretching over her to give her a hug.

"You never have to worry about that, Caden. But you have to promise me you'll never shut me out like that again. You have to let me be there for you the same way you were here for me tonight, when things are at their very worst and everything seems to be falling apart. I want to be there for you. I *need* to be there for you. And you have to promise to let me. Because I can't lose you like that again. I won't."

Caden pressed their clasped hands to his heart. "I promise," he said, a fierceness in his gaze. "I want and need that too, and I promise. I'm so sorry."

The smile she gave him was all joy and love. "Then it's you and me, 'til the end. In the darkness and in the light."

The words healed places inside him he didn't ever think would get better. "You and me, 'til the end," he repeated. And then he sat back enough to gently lay his head on her stomach. "You and me and this little guy." He pressed a kiss against her belly.

Seeing him nuzzle her stomach, with the little baby bump just starting to show, was something she'd feared she'd never get to experience. And it was so sweet it stole her breath. She gently stroked his close-shaved hair. "I'm so relieved that you're happy about the baby."

"I'm fucking ecstatic, Makenna. You two are the luckiest, best thing to ever happen to me." He eased off of her and grasped her hand again. "How far along are you?"

"Seventeen weeks on Sunday," she said, a little thrill going through her at getting to share this with him after all.

"Wow," he said, a smile dawning on his face. It brought out his dimples. "Do you know if it's a boy or a girl yet? How have you been feeling?"

"I don't know the sex yet, but my ultrasound appointment is next week. That's why I came to see you at the station. I wanted you to know about the baby so you could be involved, and I wanted to invite you to that appointment because I thought you deserved to meet your child. Aside from tonight, I've been feeling good for the past month or so. Earlier my morning sickness was terrible, but it passed." And now, talking about how she was feeling, Makenna realized that the cramps she'd had earlier had gone away. Hope flooded through her. They were going to make it out of this night after all—together and stronger for it.

"I'm sorry I wasn't there to help, Makenna, but all that changes right now," he said.

"Makenna James?" a man said as he came through the curtain. "Time for your scans."

"Oh, that didn't take too long after all," she said, ready to know just how bad her hand was and whether the bump on the head she'd gotten that'd required three stitches was anything more serious.

"Can I come?" Caden asked, standing.

"Unfortunately not, but you can wait here. She won't be gone long," the orderly said.

"Okay," Caden said, his brow furrowed. "Just give me a minute." And then he folded down the rail on her bed, leaned over her, and pulled her gently into his arms. For a long moment, he just held her. Held her so damn close. The embrace was love and life and belonging, and it eased so much of the hurt she'd been carrying around inside her. "Love you so much," he whispered. Finally, he let her go. "Sorry, I couldn't resist."

"Never be sorry for that," Makenna said with a smile as the orderly unlocked the brakes on the bed and wheeled her out of the room.

The orderly was right—the hand X-ray and head CT didn't take long. Even better, several hours later she received the news that her head scans were clean and only the first two fingers on her right hand were broken—the doctors had feared breaks throughout her hand, but it appeared to be mostly sprained. Those airbags had clearly done their job, because everyone who knew what'd happened to her repeated how lucky she was.

And every time she looked at Caden, Makenna agreed.

She drifted in and out of sleep, each time finding Caden right by her side, sometimes awake, other times asleep, his head against her hip, his hand curled around hers. Makenna didn't think she was imagining the new peacefulness he wore on his gorgeous face. Sleep had never been peaceful for him, and seeing him rest so quietly was further proof of everything he'd said.

The next time she woke up, she found her father sitting in a chair at her other side.

"Daddy," she whispered.

"Oh, Makenna. I've been trying so hard to let you sleep." He came to her side. "But I've been dying to see your eyes so I could know you were really okay," he said, so much emotion on his face. God, it was good to see him.

"I am. Or at least I will be," she said, filling him in on what the doctors had told her.

Her father blew out a deep breath and pressed a kiss to her cheek. "I hate to see you hurting."

"Don't worry," she said, his concern lodging a lump in her throat.

"Ha," he said with a wink. "Tell me how that works out for you when this little one comes."

Makenna smiled. "I suppose that's fair."

Her father's gaze dropped to where Caden slept. "So, things are…"

"Things are good, Dad. Really good. We have a lot more to talk about, but I understand what was going on and I know that we love each other. And that's all I need to know for right now. The rest we'll work out together," she said, needing her father's support.

Dad brushed a strand of hair back off her face. "Sometimes, you remind me so much of your mother. She'd be so proud of the woman you've become," he said, making her eyes well up. "You're all big heart and kind soul. And don't ever change."

"Aw, Dad," she said, her eyes leaking again.

Just then, Caden pushed into a sitting position. "Sorry I fell—" he said. His eyes went wide, and he was on his feet in an instant. "Mike. Uh, Mr. James."

"Mike is fine, son," Dad said, nailing him with a stare. "You here for my baby girl now?"

Caden nodded. Part of Makenna felt bad for him, but a bigger part of her was proud of how confident he was standing before her father. "Yes, sir. A hundred percent. When Makenna's better, I'd like to tell you what happened if you're open to it. I know how important you are to her and, well..." He nodded. "I'd just like to try to make things right."

Her father walked around the bottom of the hospital bed and came to stand in front of a much taller Caden. "It looks like you already have, but of course I'll hear what you have to say. We all will. Because you're part of the family now." Her father held out a hand, and when Caden took it, Makenna couldn't stop smiling. "Congratulations on the little one."

"Thank you, Mike. That means a lot," Caden said. Was Makenna imagining it, or were Caden's cheeks turning pink, just a little? How freaking cute was that?

"Listen, Patrick's probably climbing the walls," Dad said. "Let me head out so he can come back. They'll only allow two at a time."

"I can go so you can stay and visit," Caden said, gesturing to the door.

Her father shook his head. "Your place is right here." He clapped Caden on the back then looked at Makenna. "Get some sleep. I'll see you in a while."

"Thanks, Dad," she said.

When he left, Caden leaned against the rail of her bed and bent down to kiss her forehead. "Your father's a helluva guy."

She grinned. "Yes, he is. And so are you." Makenna only hoped that things went as well with her oldest brother.

The thought seemed to beckon him, because the next instant, Patrick walked into the room and came right up to her on the opposite side of the bed from Caden. "Makenna, Jesus. You scared the hell out of all of us." He kissed her on the forehead. "You okay?"

"Yes, I'm going to be fine. Thank you so much for coming down," she said.

"I wouldn't be anywhere else. None of us would. You know that," he said, still not acknowledging Caden. Makenna's shoulders sagged, but they had to work this out between them.

An awkward silence stretched out and Makenna was debating how to make all this right when a fluttery tingle flitted through her belly. And again.

"Oh! It's happening again," she said, grabbing Caden's hand. She flattened it against her belly. "I don't know if you'll be able to feel it but this is the second time I've felt the baby move."

Caden's face was a mask of joyful anticipation as he leaned over her. He shook his head, his smile bringing out his dimples.

"Damn," she said. "I guess we're gonna have to get used to the kid not doing things when we want him to, huh?"

Chuckling, Caden nodded. "Sounds about right."

"So, you're in this, then?" Patrick said, finally looking at Caden. "You know what, let's take this into the hall so we don't disturb Makenna."

Caden straightened and met Patrick's intense gaze eye to eye, then nodded.

"Guys, it's okay," Makenna said, worry slinking through her.

"Don't worry," Caden said, kissing her on the forehead. "We'll be right back." They disappeared into the hallway, but they didn't go so far that she couldn't hear a lot of the conversation.

"I'm *all* in," Caden said. "I know I made mistakes, but I've worked to fix them, and I won't make them again."

A long pause, and Makenna could imagine the hard-ass expression on Patrick's face. *Cop face*, she always called it. "She deserves everything, Caden." Makenna's heart melted at her brother's protectiveness.

"I couldn't agree more. And I'm going to make sure she has it. That they both do," Caden said. Just a few short hours ago, she'd worried she'd never hear Caden say something like that ever again. Now here he was, making amends with her family and holding his own. More proof of how far he'd come.

Another long pause, and she couldn't hear what they were saying.

"Yeah, well, if I do, I'll kick my own ass." Caden's voice, followed by laughter.

"You got a fucking deal," Patrick said.

A moment later, they returned to her room. "Everything okay?" she asked.

Caden and Patrick exchanged a look and a nod, and then Caden gave her a smile. "I'm here with you, Red. Everything's finally perfect."

CHAPTER TWENTY-FOUR

"This is my favorite Valentine's Day ever," Makenna said, sitting in the rocking chair as Caden drove in the last screw on the baby's crib. What could be more romantic than the father of her child whole-heartedly throwing himself into decorating the baby's nursery? They'd been working on it for hours, both of them perfectly content to just be at home together on this day that was all about celebrating love.

They'd gone with a red, yellow, and light blue color scheme and a fireman and Dalmatian dog theme. Makenna's guess had been right—they were having a boy. Caden had teared up upon seeing the ultrasound and learning the news—it was one of the sweetest things Makenna had ever seen.

Caden's smile brought out his dimples. "Oh, yeah? Me too."

She popped a piece of chocolate from a big box he'd given her into her mouth, and looked around at what used to be Caden's spare bedroom. She'd moved into his house the week after she'd been released from the hospital. Caden had insisted, and Makenna had fallen in love with him even more for how much he'd been doting on her.

"There," he said. "All done." He rose and slid the crib into place against the wall, then settled the mattress inside.

"It's coming together so nicely," she said, looking up at the mobile with its hanging fireman's helmet, Dalmatian, fire hydrant, and fire truck. "Such a cute room."

"I have an idea." Caden disappeared for a moment and returned with the stuffed bear she'd gotten him all those months ago. "I think this guy should go in here. The baby's very first bear. A gift from his mom and his dad."

"Have I told you lately how sweet you are?" she asked as he placed it in the crib.

He gave her a sheepish smile and knelt in between Makenna's thighs. "Our son deserves everything." He pressed a kiss to her belly—she wasn't very big yet, but there was no mistaking that she was pregnant. "And so do you."

She rubbed her hand over her short hair. "We all do," she said. "And we have it."

Leaning closer, Caden cupped her cheek and kissed her, a slow press of lips and a soft slide of tongues. "You taste fucking delicious," he said.

"I do?" she whispered, her arms wrapping around his neck.

He nodded and deepened the kiss. Then he tracked kisses from her cheek to her jaw to her ear.

"Watching you being all handy and domestic is really hot," she said, smiling.

He chuffed out a laugh against her neck. "Like that, do you?"

"A lot," she nodded.

"Any time you want me to hammer, drill, or screw, you just let me know," he said.

Makenna laughed. "I want those all the time, Caden. Don't you know?"

A mischievous grin on his face, he rose and pulled her up with him. Kissing her again, he walked them out of the nursery and into their bedroom. Boxes of her stuff lined one wall—slowly, but surely, they were getting her settled in. "Tell me what you want." His dark eyes blazed at her.

"You," she said, pulling her shirt over her head. "Just you."

He kissed her shoulder, the swell of her breast, her nipple through her bra. "You have me," he said. "You always have." He unclasped her bra and flicked his tongue over one nipple than the other.

Before long, they were both naked and Caden was pressing her back onto the bed. He dropped to his knees and pushed her thighs apart. The look on his face was pure masculine hunger as he leaned in. He kissed her thighs, her hip bone, the skin just above her pubic hair, driving her crazy and making her need him even more. And then he pressed a firm kiss against her clit, and Makenna couldn't help but thrust her hips.

"You want me to put my mouth on you here?" he asked, his breath ghosting over her most sensitive skin.

"God, yes," she said, looking down her body at him. He was so fucking sexy, his big shoulders filling up the space between her thighs, that harsh face peering at her with such intensity.

"Say it," he said. "Tell me what you want."

"I want you to make me come with your mouth," she rasped.

"Fuck, yes," he said, and then he was on her. Licking, sucking, relentless, driving her out of her mind. He penetrated her with one thick finger, then with another, his fingers moving inside her as he sucked hard on her clit and flicked it with his tongue. His lip piercing pressed against her flesh, a feeling that always drove her wild.

Makenna cried out and grasped his head, holding him to her, pressing him down. "God, I'm going to come already."

He growled his approval and sucked her harder, faster.

She held her breath as her orgasm washed over her in wave after wave. "Holy shit," she rasped.

"Again," he said, a mischievous glint in his eye, his pierced eyebrow arched. He angled his fingers inside her and hit a place that sent her flying.

"Jesus," she rasped. "That's so freaking good."

As he worked his fingers deep inside, he flicked his tongue over her clit hard and fast. He reached his other hand up her body and grasped her breast, his fingers stroking and squeezing her sensitive nipple. Makenna's body wound back up fast, arousal and lust and love lancing through her for this man. This gorgeous, sweet, damaged man. Her Caden.

"So good, so good, so good," she said, her hips moving, her heart racing.

"Come on my tongue, Makenna," Caden gritted out. "I want it."

The need and arousal in his tone shoved her closer to the edge. And then he angled his fingers to stroke that spot inside her again and again.

She came on a scream, her body shaking and the room spinning. Turned out that pregnant sex had some fun benefits—she found it easier to have multiple orgasms and they were so much more intense. Makenna reached her hands out to Caden.

He crawled up over her and pushed her up against the pillows until he could settle between her parted legs. "Love you so fucking much," he said, taking himself in hand. He leaned down and kissed her, an urgent kiss filled with heat and love and need, and then his cock was right there and sliding deep.

"Love you, too," Makenna moaned, arching beneath him. Hearing him say that would never get old. Finding him in that elevator had been such a gift.

Arms braced on either side of her shoulders, Caden's hips moved in a slow, grinding rhythm. His gaze dropped down to where he disappeared inside her. "Looks so fucking hot," he rasped. "Feels so good inside you."

She ran her hands down his strong sides to his ass, his muscles clenching beneath her grip. "Harder," she whispered, needing more of him, needing all of him.

"Don't wanna hurt you," he said.

"You won't," she said. "Need you so much."

"Jesus," he said, coming down all the way on top of her. His hands slid beneath her ass, tilting her hips, and then his hips were flying—hard, fast, delicious. Every impact ground against her clit until Makenna was panting and digging her fingers into his shoulders. "You own me, Red. Do you know that?" he whispered against her ear. "There isn't a part of me that isn't yours completely."

The words squeezed her heart and made her soul fly. "I feel the same way, Caden. You're everything to me."

"Fuck," he growled, his hips moving faster. "It's too good."

She wrapped her legs around his hips and dug her heels into his ass. "Come in me. I want to feel it."

He circled his hips, the new sensation suddenly pushing her closer to orgasm. "Oh, God."

"Yeah?"

"Don't stop," she whispered. "Don't stop."

"You gonna come for me again?" he asked, kissing her ear.

All she could do was moan as sensation twisted faster and faster low in her belly.

"Aw, so fucking tight," he rasped.

And then she was crying out and coming, her body gripping his.

"Yes, Makenna, yes. I'm coming. Coming so fucking hard," he said, his voice low and gritty. His cock pulsed inside her as his hips slowed and jerked.

When their bodies calmed, he eased from inside her and rolled them over until she was laying half on top of him, his arm around her shoulder and holding her close.

"I never thought I would have all this, Makenna," he said, kissing her forehead. "It's more than I ever hoped for." He tilted her chin up so he could look her in the eyes, eyes that were lighter and more unburdened than she'd ever seen them. Since they'd moved in together, he'd told her everything he'd done to get himself healthier while they'd been apart. And she was so proud of him, proud that he'd had the courage to look all that darkness in the face and still manage to find the light. "*You're* more than I ever hoped for."

She stroked her hand over his scar, her chest so full of love for this man she wasn't sure how she contained it inside her. "I'm going to spend the rest of my life making you happy."

He pressed her hand to his mouth and kissed her palm. "You know what, Red? You already do."

CHAPTER TWENTY-FIVE

5 Months Later

"Oh, Makenna, he's healthy and beautiful and just perfect," Dr. Lyons said as their son made his entrance into the world. The baby cried, and the sound crawled right into Caden's heart and made it fuller than it'd ever been in his whole life. How had he gotten so lucky?

"Good job, Makenna," Caden said, pressing a kiss to her damp cheek. "You did it. I'm so proud of you."

"He's here," Makenna said, clutching Caden's hand. "He's really here."

The doctor laid the baby on Makenna's belly and clipped off the umbilical cord while a nurse dried him off and put a striped cap on his little head. And, God, he was so little. Little and beautiful and amazing.

"Would you like to do the honors?" the doctor asked Caden, holding the scissors out to him.

"Yeah?" Caden asked, smiling. Makenna grinned and nodded, and Caden cut the cord, bringing his son fully into the world.

Finished rubbing him down, the nurse covered the baby with a blanket and lifted him higher so Makenna could hold him in her arms. Seeing Makenna hold their son for the first time was something he would never forget. He shook his head as he looked at the two of them, just so filled with awe. This...this was his family. Leaning over, he stroked her hair. "He's beautiful."

"He really is," she said, her voice shaky. "Hi, Sean, it's so nice to finally meet you."

Caden gently cupped his hand around Sean's little head. Sean David James Grayson. It was a big name for such a little guy, but they'd both fallen in love with it as a way to recognize the important people in their lives—his brother, the paramedic who'd saved Caden, and Makenna's family. Wherever they were, Caden hoped his mom and brother would be proud.

The nurse gave the three of them wrist bands and took the baby's footprint and weighed him, and then asked, "Would you like to try to feed him, Makenna?"

"Yes," she said, her face lighting up. It took a couple of tries, but Sean caught on pretty fast. And the wonder on Makenna's face was so fucking sweet that it made Caden's chest ache.

Caden held the boy's tiny hand, the little fingers curling around one of Caden's. And it gave him the best idea. Because today he was making this family official. He had the ring and the approval of her father and brothers—even Ian, who finally seemed to have warmed up to the idea of Makenna being with Caden—and now was the perfect time.

After a while, the baby pulled away and fussed, and Makenna nuzzled him, cooing and talking until the boy calmed down. For long moments, she and his son just stared at one another as she spoke quietly to him. Watching them, Caden had never felt happier or more grateful in his whole life.

"Your turn to hold him," she said, smiling up at him.

Caden's heart tripped into a sprint. Sean's little body barely filled the crook of Caden's arm. He was so little, so vulnerable, so beautiful, with a head of silky brown hair peeking out from beneath the cap and blue eyes that Caden hoped stayed that color. Part him and part her.

When the baby started to cry, Caden shook him gently in his arms and walked in a slow circle by the bed. "You and me are going to be good friends, little man. I'm going to teach you everything. I love you," he said, "you and your mom both."

The baby's little arm escaped from the blanket, and when Caden had his back to Makenna, he slipped the ring from his pocket and put it in the baby's palm. Sean's fingers closed tightly around it. "You can do the honors for me," he whispered, then he turned to Makenna, nervousness suddenly racing through him. "He's perfect, Makenna," Caden said, laying the baby on her chest again. "And I think he has a gift for you."

She gave Caden a questioning smile and grasped Sean's hand. The diamond glinted and Makenna gasped as she slipped it from his little grasp. "Oh, Caden."

Heart in his throat, he went to one knee beside her hospital bed and took her left hand in his. "Makenna James, you are everything I want and need in this world. I love you with all my heart, and I promise to devote myself to loving you and taking care of you and building a wonderful life for you and Sean. For the three of us together, as a family. You are the best thing that ever happened to me, and I would be the happiest man in the world if you would agree to be my wife. Makenna, will you marry me?"

"Yes," she said. "Oh, Caden, Yes."

Caden took the ring and slid it on her finger. Finding where he belonged in this world—and that it was with her—was a gift bigger and more meaningful than he'd ever imagined possible. He rose and kissed her, softly, sweetly, with so much love.

"I'm the luckiest man who ever lived. Thanks to you." He kissed Makenna again, then kissed Sean's head. "And you, too."

Makenna smiled even as her baby blues filled with happy tears. "I love you, Caden. So much."

Caden smiled back, his heart so damn full. "Aw, Red. I love you, too. Forever."

Read on for a sneak peek at Laura's sexy and suspenseful new series, beginning with *Ride Hard*...

The Raven Riders MC
Brotherhood. Club. Family.
They live and ride by their own rules.
These are the Raven Riders . . .

RIDE HARD

CHAPTER ONE

To say that Haven Randall's escape plans were not going as she'd hoped was quite possibly the understatement of the century. Especially since she wasn't at all sure her current situation was any better than the one she'd run from three weeks before.

But today could be the day she found that out for sure.

Staring out the window through the slats of the blinds, Haven watched as another group of motorcycles roared into the parking lot below. They'd been coming in groups of four or five for the past hour or so. And, *God,* there were a lot of them. Not surprising, since she was currently holed up at the compound of the Raven Riders Motorcycle Club. A shiver raced over her skin.

"Don't worry," Haven's friend Cora Campbell said. Sitting on the bed, back against the wall, her choppy, shoulder-length blond hair twisted up in a messy bun, Cora gave Haven a reassuring smile.

"I don't know what I'd do without you," Haven said. And it was the truth. Without Cora's bravery, encouragement, and fearless you-only-live-once attitude, Haven never would've put her longtime pipe dream of escaping from her father's house into action. Of course, those actions had landed her here, among a bunch of strange bikers of questionable character and intent, and Haven didn't know what to make of that. Yet.

But it had to be better than what would've happened if she'd stayed in Georgia. She had to believe that. *Had to.*

"Well, you won't ever have to find out," Cora said, flipping through an old gossip magazine that had been on the nightstand. "Because you're stuck with me."

"I wouldn't want to be stuck with anyone else," Haven said in a quiet voice.

Outside, the late-day sun gleamed off the steel and chrome of the motorcycles slowly but surely filling the lot. The bass beat of rock music suddenly drummed against the floor of their room. Now the Ravens' clubhouse, the building where they'd been staying for just over two weeks now had apparently once been an old mountain inn. Their rooms were on the second floor, where guests used to stay, and though Cora had been more adventurous, Haven had stayed in her room as much as possible since they'd arrived. And that was while the majority of the guys had been away from their compound on some sort of club business.

Men's laughter boomed from downstairs.

Haven hugged herself as another group of bikers tore into the lot. "There are so many of them."

Cora tossed the magazine aside and climbed off the bed. She was wearing a plain gray tank top and a pair of cutoff shorts that Bunny, an older lady who was married to one of the Ravens, had lent her. Haven's baggy white T-shirt and loose khaki cargo pants were borrowed, too. They'd run away with a few articles of clothes and cash that Haven had stolen from her father, but they'd lost all of that—and their only vehicle—two weeks ago. She and Cora literally had nothing of their own in the whole world.

Haven's belly tossed. Being totally dependent on anyone else was the last thing she wanted. She was too familiar with all the ways that could be used against her to make her do things she didn't want to do.

Standing next to her at the window, Cora said, "We're not prisoners here, Haven. We're their guests. Remember what Ike said."

Haven nodded. "I know." She hadn't forgotten. Ike Young was the member of the Ravens who had brought them there, who'd told them they were welcome to stay as long as they needed to, who said that no one would give them any trouble. Who said the Ravens helped people like them all the time.

People like them.

So, people like someone who'd grown up as the daughter of the head of a criminal organization? Someone who'd been homeschooled starting in tenth grade so her father could control her every move—and make sure she never saw her first and only boyfriend again? Someone whose father used her for a maid and a cook and planned to barter her off in a forced marriage to another crime family to cement an alliance? Someone who, after managing a middle-of-the-night escape, ended up being captured by a drug-dealing gang seven hundred miles away—a gang that had apparently received notice of a reward for capture from her father? Someone who was then rescued by soldiers and bikers at war with that gang?

Because that was Haven's reality, and she really doubted the Ravens had helped people like her before. Or, at least, she hoped not. Because she wouldn't wish the life she'd lived so far on her worst enemy.

And, *God*, was it possible her father was still looking for her? Was it possible that others, motivated by that reward, were hunting her, too? Her stomach got a sour, wiggly feeling that left her feeling nauseous.

"I'm okay," she said, giving Cora another smile. "Really." Maybe if she kept reassuring Cora of that, she'd begin to believe it herself.

"Listen, it's almost seven. Bunny said there'd be a big celebratory dinner tonight to welcome everyone back. Let's go down." Cora's bright green eyes were filled with so much enthusiasm and excitement.

Haven hated nothing more than disappointing her friend—her *only* friend, really. The only one who hadn't given up on her when Haven had been forced to drop out of school in tenth grade. Cora's father occasionally worked for Haven's, which had paved the way for Cora to be allowed to visit and even sleep over. Haven had lived for those visits, especially when her father's tight control hadn't let up even after she'd turned eighteen. Or twenty-one.

"I don't know, Cora. Can you just bring me some food later?" Haven asked, dubious that her appetite was going to rebound but knowing Cora liked taking care of her, running interference for her, protecting her. Despite how tense things had been at her father's house, Cora had slept over more and more in the time before they'd finally run. Because she'd known it had cheered Haven up so much. "I'm not hungry right now anyway."

"Oh," Cora said. "You know what? I'm not that hungry, either. I'll just wait." Her stomach growled. Loudly.

Haven stared at her, and they both chuckled. "Just go," Haven said. "Don't stay here because I'm too chicken to be around a bunch of strangers. Really. I'm so used to being alone. You know I don't mind."

Cora frowned. "That's exactly why I don't like leaving you."

"I'll feel bad if you stay. Go. Eat, visit, and meet everybody. Maybe … maybe I'll come down later," she said. Yeah. Maybe after the dinner was over, she could sneak down to the kitchen and help Bunny clean up. That might allow her to get a feel for some of the club members without being right in the middle of them, without feeling like she was under a microscope with everyone looking at her and wondering about her.

Grasping her hand, Cora's gaze narrowed. "Are you sure? You know I don't mind hanging out."

"Totally sure." Besides, Haven couldn't help but feel like she held Cora back. Cora was adventurous and outgoing and pretty much down for anything at any time, which was one of the main reasons Haven was here and not in Georgia married to a horrible stranger. But now Cora was on the run, too, though every time Haven expressed guilt about that, Cora told her it was better than waitressing at the truck stop back home and watching her father drink too much. "I might actually take a nap anyway. I didn't sleep great last night …" Because Bunny had told them all the bikers would be returning to the club today.

Cora just nodded. She didn't have to ask Haven to explain. She knew her too well. "Okay, well, I'll bring food back later. But come down if you think you can. Even for a few minutes. Okay?"

"Yup." Haven sat on the edge of the bed and threw a wave when Cora looked back over her shoulder. The door clicked shut behind her friend. On a huff, Haven flopped backwards against the hard mattress. Why couldn't she be more like Cora? Or, at least, more normal?

Because what did gaining her freedom mean if she was too scared to ever actually live?

Dare Kenyon should've been happy—or at least content. The huge fight his club had joined with the team of Special Forces Army veterans operating out of Baltimore's Hard Ink Tattoo was over, those who'd been responsible for killing two of his brothers were either dead or in custody, and all Dare's people were here at the compound, safe and sound and partying it up like tomorrow might never come.

Which made sense, since today was all anyone was ever guaranteed to get.

Standing at the far end of the carved wooden bar in the club's big rec room, Dare contemplated the tumbler of whiskey in his hand. Tilting it from side to side, he watched the amber liquid flow around the ice, the dim lighting reflecting off the facets in the cut glass. Around him, his brothers busted out in laughter as rock music filled the room with a pulsing beat. Couples danced and drank and groped. In shadowy corners here and there, people were pairing up, making out, getting hot enough to find a room upstairs. Hell, some of them didn't mind witnesses, either.

Finally, Dare tossed back a gulp of whiskey, savoring the biting heat as it seared down his throat.

"Hey, Dare." A woman with curly blond hair, a deep V-neck, and huge heels stepped up to the counter beside him. She ordered a drink from Blake, one of the prospects working the bar tonight, then turned her big smile and a generous eyeful of her cleavage toward Dare.

"Carly," he said, giving her a nod and already considering whether he was interested in what she no doubt was about to offer. He'd been with her a few times, though not much lately, since it had become more and more clear she was holding out hope to be his Old Lady.

"I'm sure glad you all are back," she said, sidling closer until she was leaning against him, her breasts against his arm, her hand rubbing his back. She was pretty, but she was also a sweet thing, the club's nickname for the attractive women who partied at the clubhouse and hung out at their track on race nights, seeking attention from and offering themselves to the brothers. Dare didn't mind having friends like Carly in the community, but he knew her interest was as much in being a part of the MC scene as it was in him. At thirty-seven, he wasn't sure he was ever going to settle down with one woman, but if he did, it certainly wasn't going to be with someone half his brothers had enjoyed, too.

And, anyway, he wasn't looking.

Dare just nodded to Carly as she pressed her way in closer until the whole front of her was tight against his side. Her hands wandered to his chest, his ass, his dick. Her lips ghosted over his cheek. "I missed you." Her hand squeezed his growing erection through his jeans. "Missed you a lot."

"Did you, now?" he said, taking another swig of Jack. The friction of her hand was luring him out of his head, out from under the strain of being responsible for so many people. It was an honor, one he'd built his life around, but he felt the weight of it some days more than others. Losing Harvey and Creed almost two weeks before, he felt that weight like a motherfucker. Hell if every new loss in his life didn't whip up his guilt from the first two...

Sonofabitch.

Carly combed her fingers through the length of his brown hair, pushing it back off his face so she could whisper into his ear. "I did. Would you like me to show you how much?" Her fingers slowly worked at his zipper, tugging him from his thoughts.

Exactly what he needed. "What is it you have in mind?" He peered down at her, really appreciating the easy, lighthearted expression on her face. Nothing too deep, nothing too heavy, but full of life all the same.

Her fingers undid the button on his jeans and slipped in against his skin, finding and palming his now rigid cock. Fuck, that felt good. Warm and tight and full of promise.

Smiling, Carly slid herself in front of Dare, pinning her body between his and the hard wooden counter. Her eyes were full of heat and need. "I could drop to my knees right here. Suck you off. Let you fuck my face. Or we could go upstairs, baby. Whatever you want." With the hand not stroking him, she wrapped an arm around his neck, her fingers playing with the long strands of his hair. "You seem ... tense, upset. Let me make you feel better?"

And now, on top of everything else, he had a warm, willing woman wanting to make him forget all his troubles. So, yeah, he should've been content.

Dare emptied his glass and slammed it down on the counter. Fuck it. Grasping her face in his hand, he trailed his thumb over her bottom lip, stroking, dipping inside so she could suck on his flesh. "Always did love that mouth," he said.

She grinned around his thumb and nodded, then she slowly slid down his body.

Dare closed his eyes, wanting nothing more than to lose himself in the moment, the sensation, the physical. But his gut wouldn't stop telling him that some part of their recent troubles were going to come back and bite them in the ass. The past had a way of doing that. Which was why Dare always kept one eye trained over his shoulder. But this particular past was only days old and way bigger than their typical fights. Along with the SpecOps team operating out of Hard Ink, the Ravens had played a role in taking down longtime enemies and Baltimore's biggest heroin dealers—the Church Gang. In the process, they'd exposed an international drug smuggling conspiracy involving a team of former soldiers turned hired mercenaries and at least one three-star, active-duty general. The Ravens had initially come into the fight as hired help, but they'd soon taken up the cause as their own when Harvey and Creed had been killed.

Given all that, Dare had a really fucking hard time believing the dust would just settle and life would go back to normal without any blowback.

As Carly got into a crouched position at his feet, Dare opened his eyes and tried to shake away all the churn and burn in his head. But then his gaze snagged on a girl in the doorway across the room. Clarity stole over him, pushing away the fog of lust and the haze of troubled thoughts. The girl had the longest blond hair he'd ever seen, like some fairy-tale princess, or a fucking angel. Pale, small, almost too beautiful to look at. She stood out so starkly that it was almost as if she glowed in the dim room. Like a beacon. Bright and shiny and new.

One of these things is not like the other. And it was the timid beauty wearing too-big clothes and no makeup, hovering on the edge of the room.

And Dare wasn't the only man who noticed.

Coming April 26, 2016

ABOUT THE AUTHOR

Laura Kaye is the New York Times and USA Today bestselling author of over a twenty books in contemporary romance and romantic suspense. Laura grew up amidst family lore involving angels, ghosts, and evil-eye curses, cementing her life-long fascination with storytelling and the supernatural. Laura lives in Maryland with her husband and two daughters, and appreciates her view of the Chesapeake Bay every day.

Visit Laura Kaye at http://www.LauraKayeAuthor.com/

Follow Laura on Twitter at @laurakayeauthor

Like Laura on Facebook

ACKNOWLEDGEMENTS

As my first published book, *Hearts in Darkness* will always be special to me, which makes the publication of *Love in the Light* special, too. When I wrote *Hearts in Darkness* in 2010, I never expected to write more about Caden and Makenna. The story came to me with a happy-for-now ending that left it up to the reader's imagination what happened to them after their night in the elevator. And for a long time, that was all there was for me. I saw pieces of their future, but no story. And then one did the story came to me. I saw it all. Every up and down. And just how *far down* those downs would be. By that time, I was getting frequent questions from readers—will you ever write more about Caden and Makenna? In fact, that has been the single most frequently asked question I've received from readers over the entire course of my writing career.

And so *Love in the Light* was born.

Caden and Makenna are some of my favorite characters I've ever written, and I hope you love their journey in this book. Because this book is first and foremost for you, the readers, and I thank you from the bottom of my heart for loving these characters the way I do.

Next I need to thank my best friend and fellow writer, Lea Nolan, for encouraging me, brainstorming with me, and reading the book with such a thoughtful eye. Christi Barth, Jillian Stein, and Liz Berry also deserve thanks for reading the book and letting me know what they thought—together, you all gave me the courage to let this one out into the world. Thank you!

I must also thank my family, for making it possible for me to carve out the time to get this done. I love you all so much! ~LK

Want More Hot Contemporary Romance from Laura Kaye?

Check out:

The Raven Riders Series
Brotherhood. Club. Family.
They live and ride by their own rules.
These are the Raven Riders . . .

Ride Hard (Raven Riders #1)

Raven Riders Motorcycle Club President Dare Kenyon rides hard and values loyalty above all else. He'll do anything to protect the brotherhood of bikers—the only family he's got—as well as those who can't defend themselves. So when beautiful but mistrustful Haven Randall lands on the club's doorstep scared that she's being hunted, Dare takes her in, swears to keep her safe, and pushes to learn the secrets overshadowing her pretty smile before it's too late.

Ride Rough (Raven Riders #2)

Alexa Harmon thought she had it all—the security of a good job, a beautiful home, and a powerful, charming fiancé who offered the life she never had growing up. But when her dream quickly turns into a nightmare, Alexa realizes she's fallen for a façade she can't escape—until her ex-boyfriend and Raven Riders MC vice-president Maverick Ryland offers her a way out. Forced together to keep Alexa safe, their powerful attraction reignites and Maverick determines to do whatever it takes to earn a second chance—one Alexa is tempted to give. But her ex-fiancé isn't going to let her go without a fight, one that will threaten everything they both hold dear.

The Hard Ink Series
Five dishonored soldiers
Former Special Forces
One last mission
These are the men of Hard Ink...

Hard As It Gets (Hard Ink #1)

Trouble just walked into Nicholas Rixey's tattoo parlor. Becca Merritt is warm, sexy, wholesome—pure temptation to a very jaded Nick. He's left his military life behind to become co-owner of Hard Ink Tattoo, but Becca is his ex-commander's daughter. Loyalty won't let him turn her away. Lust has plenty to do with it too. With her brother presumed kidnapped, Becca needs Nick. She just wasn't expecting to want him so much. As their investigation turns into all-out war with an organized crime ring, only Nick can protect her. And only Becca can heal the scars no one else sees.

Hard As You Can (Hard Ink #2)

Shane McCallan doesn't turn his back on a friend in need, especially a former Special Forces teammate running a dangerous, off-the-books operation. Nor can he walk away from Crystal, the gorgeous blonde waitress is hiding secrets she doesn't want him to uncover. Too bad. He's exactly the man she needs to protect her sister, her life, and her heart. All he has to do is convince her that when something feels this good, you hold on as hard as you can—and never let go.

Hard to Hold On To (Hard Ink #2.5)

Edward "Easy" Cantrell knows better than most the pain of not being able to save those he loves—which is why he is not going to let Jenna Dean, the woman he helped rescue from a gang, out of his sight. He may have just met her, but Jenna's the first person to make him feel alive since that devastating day in the desert more than a year ago. As the pair are thrust together while chaos reigns around them, they both know one thing: the things in life most worth having are the hardest to hold on to.

Hard to Come By (Hard Ink #3)

When a sexy stranger asks questions about her brother, Emilie Garza is torn between loyalty to the brother she once idolized and fear of the war-changed man he's become. Derek DiMarzio's easy smile and quiet strength tempt Emilie to open up, igniting the desire between them and leading Derek to crave a woman he shouldn't trust. Now, Derek and Emilie must prove where their loyalties lie before hearts are broken and lives are lost. Because love is too hard to come by to let slip away…

Hard to Be Good (Hard Ink #3.5)

Hard Ink Tattoo owner Jeremy Rixey has taken on his brother's stateside fight against the forces that nearly killed Nick and his Special Forces team a year before. Now, Jeremy's whole world has been turned upside down—not the least of which by kidnapping victim Charlie Merritt, a brilliant, quiet blond man who tempts Jeremy to settle down for the first time ever. With tragedy and chaos all around them, temptation flashes hot, and Jeremy and Charlie can't help but wonder why they're trying so hard to be good…

Hard to Let Go (Hard Ink #4)

Beckett Murda hates to dwell on the past. But his investigation into the ambush that killed half his Special Forces team and ended his Army career gives him little choice. Just when his team learns how powerful their enemies are, hard-ass Beckett encounters his biggest complication yet—his friend's younger sister, seductive, feisty Katherine Rixey. When Kat joins the fight, she lands straight in Beckett's sights . . . and in his arms. Not to mention their enemies' crosshairs. Now Beckett and Kat must set aside their differences to work together, because the only thing sweeter than justice is finding love and never letting go.

Hard As Steel (Hard Ink #4.5)

After identifying her employer's dangerous enemies, Jessica Jakes takes refuge at the compound of the Raven Riders Motorcycle Club. Fellow Hard Ink tattooist and Raven leader Ike Young promises to keep Jess safe for as long as it takes, which would be perfect if his close, personal, round-the-clock protection didn't make it so hard to hide just how much she wants him—and always has. The last thing Ike needs is alone time with the sexiest woman he's ever known, one he's purposely kept at a distance for years. Now, Ike's not sure he can keep his hands or his heart to himself— or that he even wants to anymore.

Hard Ever After (Hard Ink #5)

After a long battle to discover the truth, the men and women of Hard Ink have a lot to celebrate, especially the wedding of two of their own—Nick Rixey and Becca Merritt, whose hard-fought love deserves a happy ending. But an old menace they thought long gone reemerges, threatening the peace they've only just found. Now, for one last time, Nick and Becca must fight for their always and forever.

Hard to Serve (Hard Ink #5.5)

To protect and serve is all Detective Kyler Vance ever wanted to do, so when Internal Affairs investigates him as part of the new police commissioner's bid to oust corruption, everything is on the line. Which makes meeting smart, gorgeous submissive, Mia Breslin, at an exclusive play club the perfect distraction. Their scorching scenes lure them to play together again and again. But then Kyler runs into Mia at work and learns that he's been dominating the daughter of the hard-ass boss who has it in for him. Now Kyler must choose between life-long duty and forbidden desire before Mia finds another who's not so hard to serve.

The Heroes Series

Her Forbidden Hero (Heroes #1)
Former Army Special Forces Sgt. Marco Vieri has never thought of Alyssa Scott as more than his best friend's little sister, but her return home changes that...and challenges him to keep his war-borne demons at bay. Marco's not the same person he was back when he protected Alyssa from her abusive father, and he's not about to let her see the mess he's become. But Alyssa's not looking for protection—not anymore. Now that she's back in his life, she's determined to heal her forbidden hero one touch at a time...

One Night with a Hero (Heroes #2)
After growing up with an abusive, alcoholic father, Army Special Forces Sgt. Brady Scott vowed never to marry or have kids. Sent stateside to get his head on straight—and his anger in check—Brady's looking for a distraction. He finds it in Joss Daniels, his beautiful new neighbor whose one-night-only offer for hot sex leads to more. Suddenly, Brady's not so sure he can stay away. But when Joss discovers she's pregnant, Brady's rejection leaves her feeling abandoned. Now, they must overcome their fears before they lose the love and security they've found in each other, but can they let go of the past to create a future together?

Made in the USA
Charleston, SC
08 March 2017